Praise for *A Glimmer of Death*

"There's crispness in Wesley's plotting and sparkle in the supporting characters, notably Dessa's feisty, elderly aunts—both possessed of extrasensory gifts—and a possible love interest in ex-cop Lennox Royal. There's also something oddly comforting about a black woman in fiction who isn't weighed down by societal pathology and who can appreciate a good glass of merlot and reruns of *Downton Abbey* as much as the next woman. In between heavier mystery fare, this unicorn of a black cozy is a welcome palate cleanser." —***Los Angeles Times***

"The creator of Newark private eye Tamara Hayle dials back the wisecracks and bumps up the paranormal hints to launch a new series featuring a widowed African-American Realtor whose workplace is a hot mess." —***Kirkus Reviews***

"Widow Odessa Jones, the psychically gifted narrator of this strong series launch from Wesley, can see glimmers, aura-like colors that correspond to a person's emotional state. . . . Wesley perfectly captures her protagonist's emotions, including the lingering melancholy she feels for her late husband. . . . Readers will hope to see a lot more of kind, empathetic Odessa." —***Publishers Weekly***

Praise for Valerie Wilson Wesley's Tamara Hayle Mysteries

"There's a richness of language in Wesley's writing, joined by a delightful sense of humor. She makes the mean streets of Newark come alive." —***San Francisco Examiner***

"A major talent . . . Wesley's voice—laden with wit, style, and sparkle—is unique in mystery fiction." —***The Globe and Mail***

"[Tamara Hayle] has a way with a wisecrack that is positively lethal." —***The Washington Post Book World***

"A wonderfully believable and independent sleuth who combines intellect and intuition, sexiness and self-control."
—***The Denver Post***

"Outstanding. . . . A warm, witty comedy of midlife manners."
—***Boston Herald***

"An engaging heroine—smart, sexy, tough but tender."
—***Houston Chronicle***

"The desperate search for a missing child makes Newark PI Tamara Hayle's eighth outing a chilling, thought-provoking read. . . . Wesley recounts Tamara's struggles with equal parts irony, compassion and insight."
—***Publishers Weekly*** on *Of Blood and Sorrow*

Books by Valerie Wilson Wesley

The Odessa Jones Mystery series

A Glimmer of Death

A Fatal Glow

A Fatal Glow

Valerie
Wilson Wesley

Kensington Publishing Corp.
www.kensingtonbooks.com

KENSINGTON BOOKS are published by

Kensington Publishing Corp.
119 West 40th Street
New York, NY 10018

ISBN: 978-1-4967-2783-1 (ebook)

ISBN: 978-1-4967-2781-7

First Kensington Trade Paperback Printing: March 2022

10 9 8 7 6 5 4 3 2 1

Printed in the United States of America

For sister-friends who have been with me on every book:
Thandiwe Watts-Jones, Janet Taylor Pickett, Iqua Colson,
Sandra Roberts Bell, and Cathy Carlozzi

Acknowledgments

There are so many people who have supported me through the production of this book and the terrible year we've all been through. Thank you to my Kensington editors—Wendy McCurdy and Elizabeth Trout—and Michelle Addo and Larissa Ackerman, also at Kensington, for your support.

My continuing gratitude to Faith Hampton Childs, who I am fortunate enough to call a friend as well as an agent. My thanks and love to my family—Richard, Thembi, Nandi, Primo—for their thoughtfulness and for bringing such joy into my life. And dare I forget Junior, aka Juniper, for his small but worthy contribution!

Chapter 1

There was no whiff of nutmeg, the usual warning that death is heading my way. No signs from "the gift," that unreliable second sight that graces (and I use the word loosely) the women in my mother's family. No disturbing colors or sounds. I only heard my late husband's voice quoting, oddly enough, those well-known lines from *Macbeth:*

> *By the pricking of my thumbs,*
> *Something wicked this way comes.*

Darryl's voice usually comes at the end of a dream when I'm going through a rough spot or missing him more than usual. So why this morning? I glanced up from my laptop, as two men in suits that cost more than my monthly mortgage strolled past my cubicle into Tanya Risko's office. The younger was wickedly handsome; the older just looked wicked. His skin had a yellowish cast to it, a problem for a dark-brown-skinned man, and although he was built like an aging prizefighter, the ring had definitely won the last round. Risko Realty, where I work, is a cut-rate real estate firm. Tanya, the owner and my boss, inherited the business from a vicious man brutally murdered in the room where the two gentlemen were headed.

"Wonder what that's about," muttered Vinton Laverne, who worked in the cubicle next to mine. Our work spaces were narrow and separated by low plastic boundaries, making it easy to keep your eye on what folks were doing and poke your nose where it wasn't meant to go, something at which Vinton, a thin, dapper man, solemn as an owl, was adept. He also had a tart, endearing sense of humor that could turn bitter on a dime. When I first joined Risko Realty, he'd carried a gloomy gray glimmer that finally disappeared. He was happier now; everything about him had changed, including the glimmer.

Glimmers are something only I can see when certain people enter my space. A gift from the gift, you might say. They can be as hazy as a shadow or as bright as a colorful aura; they often give a hint of what to expect from a stranger or a clue into who that person really is. Yet they can change for better or worse depending upon what life has served up. My aunt Phoenix, an expert on glimmers, charms, spells, and all things weird and extrasensory, said that we who see glimmers give them our own interpretation so it's not only what you get from a person but who you think that person truly is—which complicates everything. Yet seeing glimmers, coupled with the ability to sense, hear, and smell things other folks can't, is what makes me unique, along with a silver streak of hair that occasionally appears on the left side of my head.

"If you want my guess, I'd say there's something going on between one of them and our little Tanya. Maybe both of them?" said Vinton with a naughty wink that brought my attention back to him. Vinton, Tanya Risko, Harley Wilde, and Louella Jefferson had all become family to me now. When I began working at Risko Realty more than a year ago, there were eight of us; now we were down to five. Terrible things had happened to us in the past, and we'd healed together, just as a family does.

Louella was our youngest member. She had a sweet baby face with rosebud lips, wide, expressive eyes, and skin as smooth and dark as bittersweet chocolate. She'd gone through rough times and they'd toughened her up, but there was still a gentleness about her. The first time I saw her, I was taken aback by her glimmer that was such a shocking shade of violet it made me want to cry. Things were better now. She still fought demons (one that would haunt her for the rest of her life), but she was trying to do the best she could, to make a way for herself in real estate. Risko Realty was a new beginning for her, as it once had been for me. Usually, she had an easy smile that popped whenever she lifted her head, but the sight of these two men had wiped it off; something had shaken her to the core.

"Everything okay?" I asked. Louella stared straight ahead, her gaze following the men as they headed into Tanya's office; then her eyes dropped down to the laptop on her desk. Were they part of her past? I knew Louella hid parts of herself that she considered shameful and tucked away trying to forget. Her old glimmer swept over her, then disappeared in nearly the same instant, and that worried me. Vinton couldn't see what I saw but knew that something was wrong.

"Do you know these two guys, Baby Doll? Did they do something to hurt you?" he asked, his voice protective and concerned. When he liked you, Vinton gave you a nickname. Mine was Sunshine, Louella's Baby Doll.

She shook her head, avoiding his eyes.

"Then why won't you look at me?"

She glanced at him, then answered his question, her voice close to a whisper. "Yeah. I know them both. Red says the old one stole his daddy's land and won't give it back. I know the young one from back in the day. Red knows him from those days, too." Red was Louella's fiancé and the father of Erika, her eight-year-old daughter. He was part of her past and now her future. Although I hadn't met him yet, she claimed he had come back into her life to redeem them both. I wasn't so sure.

"Louella, that can't be true. Charlie Risko stole Red's daddy's land," I said, stating something that we all knew now. As I spoke, I touched the talisman I wear around my neck. It's a blue lace agate on a leather string that once belonged to Rosemary, my mother, and was given to me last year by Celestine, my other "gifted" aunt. The mere mention of Charlie Risko's name called for serious spiritual protection.

"I know," Louella said, avoiding my eyes. "But Red doesn't feel that way. He feels different."

The *vroom* of a motorcycle caught my attention before I had a chance to ask just what that difference was, and my friend late-as-usual Harley Wilde bounced into the office, with a spring in his step and carrying the late-morning latte grande he never failed to bring me. Settling down in his cubicle, he pulled the lid off his coffee, blew on it, and sipped loudly.

Harley was younger than me by nearly two decades. We weren't related by blood but had become as close as kin, connecting us in ways that surprised us both. He tried to maintain a "gangsta" swagger, but it concealed a joyful spirit, caring nature, and quick grin that put even curmudgeons at ease. He'd served a stint in Afghanistan and was left with a limp and invisible wounds he never talked about—at least not to me. Like all of us here, he was building a new life, working hard, and, in his case, attending the local community college trying hard to earn a degree.

"Do you-all know who that old guy is?" he said, placing the coffee down next to his laptop and nodding toward Tanya's door. "He's been around for a while. His name is Casey Osborne, one of the richest men in town, in all Essex County, for that matter. I saw him drive up in his black Cadillac while I was standing in line at Starbucks."

"He doesn't look that old to me," Vinton said defensively. I silently agreed; the man was roughly my age if you added a few years. "But I do agree that Cadillacs age you. They went out with minks."

"I hope Tanya's being careful." Harley picked up his coffee again, took another sip. "She said something to me last week about finding a new business partner and making some new investments. Hope it's not with that guy."

"He's not in the Mob, is he?" Genuine concern crossed Vinton's face.

"No, he's too smart for that, but the young one, the guy who is with him? I don't know much about him, except his name, Tyler Chase. I've seen him hanging with guys you don't want to cross. The kind of dudes who would sooner cut your throat than say hello. He's a hustler, been a hustler since he got out of high school, and I do know a hustler when I see one. I've seen enough of them in my day."

"Yeah, like in the mirror," Vinton said teasingly, which made Harley scowl but then chuckle good-naturedly. "You're right about that old man. Been there. Seen that. You'd think Tanya would have learned how to watch her money around men who mean her no good. She should know better by now. We all should have learned that lesson," he said more to himself than to any of us. Vinton shook his head and gave a somber sigh; Louella closed her eyes as if blocking disturbing thoughts. I kept mine to myself.

Lively laughter and loud talking poured from Tanya's office, filling our small space with boisterous sound, bringing my aunt Phoenix's words to mind. *Just plain piggish.* That was what she called big men who took up more food, drink, or space on buses and in life than they were entitled to. And these guys with their noisy presence and boisterous laughter struck me as just that. I didn't know who they were, but there was something not quite trustworthy about them. Or maybe it was simply Darryl's words coming back to me as they had. Yet with the exception of Louella, Harley knew Tanya longer and better than any of us. Maybe he knew more than he was saying.

I'm still not sure what to make of Tanya Risko, who had certainly changed in the year I'd known her. She'd inherited not only Risko Realty from Charlie Risko, her horror of a husband, but also his ill-gotten property and shady investments that made her a very wealthy woman, quite different from the battered young soul I'd first met. She was a good-looking girl, tall, thin, stylish with an obsession for rich ladies' clothes that cost a workingwoman's weekly salary. Her skin was tawny brown, darker or lighter depending on the time she spent in the sun. She slipped with ease into any world she deemed fashionable—be it white, black, or brown—to bask in the glory of being young and rich in a town where most folks were neither.

"Us widows need to stick together," Tanya had said to me the day after her husband's death, which knocked the stuffing out of me and took me a full minute to catch my breath. Yet Tanya was also capable of generosity, paying for the funeral of a coworker who had taken her own life. When we'd met, Tanya had seemed a dreamy girl-child saddled with an abusive husband and low self-esteem. I was glad to see she was coming into her own, but I wasn't quite sure what that "own" meant. So I stirred her carefully with a long-handled spoon, as Aunt Phoenix would put it—well enough to mix but not get burned. The girl had *no* glimmer as far as I could tell, which according to my aunt didn't necessarily mean that something was missing. But two men whom she'd been intimately involved with had met sudden violent ends. Some folks might simply call that bad luck; I hoped that was all it was.

I thought of that now as she left her office chatting and chuckling with the older of the two men. Louella dropped her head low and stared at her hands as they approached. Vinton impishly whistled "The Imperial March" from *The Empire Strikes Back.* Harley, cool as ever, leaned back in his chair sipping his coffee. I forced my lips into an uncomfortable smile.

"Casey, this is the lady I was telling you about. Here she is, working hard right in my little office, can you imagine that? Well, anyway. This is Mrs. Dessa Jones and she is a chef and the owner of D&D Delights, and I know she would love to cater your classy brunch for next Sunday. She'll be doing me a big personal favor, won't you, Dessa?" Tanya's voice, sweet and chirpy, made me fear the worst. She grabbed a chair, pulling it into my cubicle so the man could sit down. "Casey told me he thinks he knew you from high school, that you knew his wife, so I guess you-all go back. Listen, I'm going to leave you to talk business. Thanks, Case. Thanks, my dear Mrs. Jones. And don't let him shortchange you," she added with a wink.

Tanya had added the "Mrs. Jones" bit in the little-girl voice she pulled out when she needed my favor or support; apparently, she needed both. The wink said the man had money, a not-so-subtle reminder that I hadn't had a sale in two months. It also said she was offering me a chance to fix my broken water heater and I'd better not blow it.

"Glad to be of service, Mr. Osborne," I said. Despite the warmer weather, I couldn't forget those cold showers. I'd complained so often that Vinton had finally offered me his, and I'd taken him up on it yesterday morning.

Casey Osborne raised his eyebrow slightly and studied me like a bird contemplating a wriggling caterpillar. "It's too damn tight in here," he said, shifting his weight around in my small space to show how uncomfortable he was. "These damn cramps are about to kill me even with all those meds I keep getting, don't do nothing but make me want to sleep." He paused for a moment to yawn loudly. "You really don't remember me, do you?"

I looked harder, noticing again his pale, sweaty face, and I tried to imagine him younger and thirty pounds thinner. He had an odd smell about him, too, and I wondered if the gift was trying to tell me something.

"Well, I know Tanya said that I knew your wife, but—"

He threw back his head and laughed, louder than he needed to as if I'd said something funny. "Wow! You really *don't* recognize me, do you? You don't remember the kids in high school shouting my name from the stands during those games? They called me Case then. Like 'stay on the case, Case.' Stay on the case . . ." He kept repeating the phrase as if that would jar my memory.

"Oh, yes," I said, studying him again, as everything about those miserable years came back in a rush: the high school I hated, the kids who hated me, and Case, the king of the place—who had just squeezed his hulking frame into my tiny cubicle. "I knew your wife, Aurelia," I added, remembering her part in my unpleasant history.

"Ex-wife! Shook off that mean, crazy witch as soon as I could," he quickly corrected me. "My new wife is Mona, pretty name, pretty girl. You wouldn't have known her; she's younger than the two of you," he added unnecessarily. I nodded absent-mindedly, but my mind had gone back to Aurelia, the first one, a few years older than me, who had been my only friend, and had never been crazy or evil as far as I could remember.

I spent a year and a half at Grovesville High. My father was between jobs, and my mother worked as a librarian in a nearby town. We stayed with Aunt Phoenix until we could find an apartment. She'd just bought her tiny house and filled it with hanging herbs and other plants that made my father sneeze and my mother's eyes water, which made her look like she was always weeping. I'm not sure if it was the high school, my mother's tears, or being a moody teenager that made my life so unbearable. I suspect Aunt Phoenix with her eccentric ways didn't help.

And that was what endeared me to Aurelia, who was also saddled with an offbeat (to put it kindly) aunt who had recently moved to Grovesville from the Dominican Republic. Aunt Dahina would pick Aurelia up after cheerleading practice with the haughty airs of a 1930s movie star in her ancient, fume-spewing Oldsmobile that smelled up the road. Aurelia must have recognized a kindred suffering spirit in me and took me under her wing, no small thing for a senior to do for a freshman, particularly since Case Osborne was her boyfriend. I didn't like him; I knew that the moment I met him. I never understood what Aurelia saw in him, but it must have been something big, because they stayed together after high school and eventually married.

"So how is Aurelia these days?" I asked because I honestly wanted to know.

He answered with a shrug. "See as little of her as possible. Been divorced for years. I'm working on getting full custody of my son as soon as possible."

I studied him closely when he said that, thankful she was no longer with him, but also realizing that nothing about him had changed. Even his glimmer was the same as it had been in high school, although at the time I didn't know what it was because nobody bothered to explain. My mother avoided mentioning our gift, and Aunt Phoenix kept her knowledge to herself. Casey Osborne's glimmer was a bluish brown, a disconcerting shadow that made me instinctively pull away from him just as I used to. Except now I knew what it was.

He had been a nasty teenager full of so much arrogance it left no room for anything else, including Aurelia, who worshiped him like a god. And she wasn't the only one. Casey Osborne ran the school; his prowess on the football field made up for his cruelty to other students. He collected young girls' hearts like football trophies, lying and cheating to get his way. His callous indifference drove one poor teenage girl to suicide. Or so it was said. Her death dimmed his star for a week, but nobody held him responsible and after the initial mourning period was over the girl was quickly forgotten. It seemed to make no difference to Aurelia at all, which I never understood. It certainly did to me, and that must have shown on my face.

"I see you remember me?" he said, grinning wildly, misinterpreting my expression. "So I went from high school, big-time scholarship to college, into business, where, I guess folks would say, I made some killings," he added, answering a question I hadn't asked.

"No doubt."

He gave me a crooked, curious smile, then moved on. "So the wife, Mona, will be calling you with details about the brunch, okay?"

I said nothing for a beat, then remembered the chill of this morning's cold shower. "Okay."

"One thing the wife will probably forget to tell you, though, is about my son. She's beautiful but forgetful. Lacey is seriously allergic to nuts, walnuts, peanuts, nuts period. He will definitely be there, so don't fix anything with nuts. Nothing. Here, this is a picture of him so you'll know him when you see him." He pulled up a picture of a teenage boy on his cell and thrust it in front of me. "He's my boy, though he doesn't look nothing like his dad. She, the witch, will come with him, so they'll be there together."

"He does look like Aurelia. He has her pretty eyes," I said, remarking on what I could see of them. The boy looked half-asleep, as if awakened for a photograph he didn't want to take.

Osborne shrugged as if he'd never noticed. Aurelia's eyes or not, Lacey was no heartbreaker like his father had once been. The boy's face was scarred by adolescent acne, and his T-shirt fell sloppily off his large frame. His fake smile revealed a mouth filled with braces that had probably cost his father a fortune.

"What he lacks in looks he makes up in brains. The wife is pregnant. A boy, they tell me," he said with a proud grin, as if expecting me to congratulate him because the new one's looks would outshine those of the other. "By the way, there will be a lot of important folks there on Sunday, and if Mrs. Risko is right about you, more work should come your way. The wife will take care of the contract and whatever else you need."

He didn't offer a handshake, and I was grateful he didn't, but tossed two embossed cream-colored business cards on my desk instead. Without saying anything else, he scraped his chair loudly on the floor as he pushed it out of my cubicle and headed back to Tanya's office.

"Watch yourself, Sunshine," Vinton muttered when Osborne was out of earshot.

"Tanya's the one who better watch herself," Harley added, slurping the last of his coffee. Louella, turning back to her computer, said nothing. The smell of nutmeg left me frozen in my chair.

Chapter 2

I should have seen it coming. The signs were certainly there: the sudden whiff of nutmeg when Osborne left my cubicle; Darryl's voice coming in the morning as it did. The gift was whispering that death was headed my way, and I simply didn't hear it. Maybe I was still recovering from that morning's shower that left me so cold I couldn't pee or Osborne squeezing his bulk into my tiny space or "the wife's" snooty directions for a "classy brunch" (whatever the heck that was). There just hadn't been enough space in my overworked brain for the gift's cryptic messages so I was caught with my drawers down, as Aunt Phoenix would bluntly put it.

My conversation with Mrs. Osborne began on an unfortunate note. *Don't expect suggestions from me. I'm not some ignorant cook*, she said when she called me after her husband left. (Good thing she couldn't see my eyes roll to the back of my head.) The conversation slid downhill from there. Any guests with seafood allergies? I asked. *Don't know, just label everything so we won't be sued. And no meat*, she said. *Go light on salt. I mostly drink smoothies so I won't gain weight and try to always eat healthy. I won't be eating.* No mention of her stepson's nut allergy! The man knew his wife. *I expect you to take care of everything else. I will show up late in my pretty little dress with my pretty little smile.* (Good thing she couldn't see my lips do a lemon-sucking pucker.) How many guests are you expecting? *Thirty. Our house is very large, the living room vast. I'll e-mail you a photograph of the space so you'll know what to expect.* (So much for modesty!) What time is the event? *Noon to four.* I thought irritably, *Too late for a brunch.* The rentals will be delivered Saturday, which is when I'll set things up, I said. I'll need to come early on Sunday morning to do last-minute warm-ups, arrange platters, and— *Just don't wake me up,* she broke in, cutting me off. So I'll need to rent tables, tablecloths, chairs, dishes, platters, silverware, napkins, glasses? *Rent whatever you need to rent, but bring things in through the back door in the kitchen. I don't want to see anybody. We'll take care of the liquor, bar, and bartender.* This is such short notice, and with all the rentals and everything, I'll need to charge you a hundred dollars a head, I said, my voice veering close to a whine. *I don't give a damn. I don't care about the money. Make it one hundred fifty, for all I care. This is his thing, not mine. He gave you his card. Fax him the contract. Use it!* Done at one hundred fifty dollars for thirty guests! I said, and hung up before she could change her mind. Then I leaned back in my chair, thanking the universe and those hovering spirits who mean me well, wrote an agreement, signed it, and faxed it to Osborne.

That was when my nosy coworkers threw in their two cents' worth.

"One hundred fifty bucks each for thirty people? Sunshine, you've come a long way from free chocolate chip cookies. You are kicking behind with your catering self! How much money you going to make?" asked Vinton, rubbing his palms together. "Forty-five hundred bucks! You'll have it made in the shade, girl, as one of my old-timey boyfriends used to say. Do they need a bartender? Please tell me they do, and I'll be there with my starched white shirt and fawning grin. You know I make a mean martini!"

"That's a lot of cooking, Dessa, a lot of serving. You need to get a lot of stuff done before Sunday. How will you handle all that?" asked Harley.

"Thanks for the vote of confidence."

"No, I mean it. You're going to need some serious help," he added, his voice filled with concern.

He was right! I was struck dumb. The reality of what I'd just done suddenly smacked me in the face. I scrolled nervously through the photographs of a million-dollar house filled with million-dollar stuff. No doubt, they were expecting a million-dollar brunch that was worthy of the house. Classy, as the woman had said, and now I knew what she meant, and that was not D&D Delights—not at this point anyway. The walls of the "vast" living room were hung with abstract paintings of things I couldn't identify that I suspected cost more money than I wanted to know. Angular "modern" sculptures that looked like they belonged on the moon were placed strategically throughout the room. An elegant staircase, obviously meant for floating down, snaked its way from the upper floors to the French doors leading into the living room. Sunlight poured in through the many picture windows. I could only imagine what the kitchen looked like.

It would take big-time planning to pull off an event in a place like this. I hadn't tackled anything this fancy since Darryl left me. The most I'd done were cakes, cookies, and pies—easy stuff. Darryl and I had been a team, and the event itself was almost an afterthought—except for the money, of course. He did the planning—figuring how to use the space, writing the contracts, finding the rentals, dealing with setup and cleanup crews, and I had all the fun—planning, cooking, tasting. (Darryl did some of that, too.) We'd done a dinner for forty a few months before he died and pulled it off in high style. From soup to nuts—in our case, black-eyed pea soup to peach cobbler—all of it had gone like clockwork, as well choreographed as an Alvin Ailey dance performance. Now everything had changed.

"You okay, Dess?" asked Harley, peering into my cubicle.

"Overwhelmed." I uttered the only word that captured how I felt. Harley dragged a chair into my cubicle to sit beside me.

"Not depressed, scared, angry, just overwhelmed?"

I nodded like a woeful child.

"Overwhelmed is easy. I can fix that."

"How?"

"Listen. I'm up to doing anything you need me to. Cook. Carry. Serve. Name it. I owe you. Big-time."

I nodded, grateful, but could no more imagine Harley Wilde donning an apron than I could envision him in tights and a tutu.

This was my business; I was on my own. If I was going to keep D&D Delights going, I had to find a way to do *all* the things a professional caterer was expected to do. "I'll be fine," I said, giving what I hoped was a confident smile. I picked up a pen and began scribbling down what I needed to do: rentals, menu, cooking, pre-event setup, plating, serving, post-event cleanup . . . I stopped, abruptly laying my pen back down on my desk.

Was I delusional? Why did I sign that contract? Had that cold shower I took this morning frozen my brain? How could I do this by myself—to myself? D&D Delights was not what we'd planned it to be; I needed Darryl for that. What kind of a fool was I? I should call Osborne immediately and tell him that I had to cancel, plead with him, convince him that I'd made a mistake. A close relative had just had a heart attack. I'd come down with a disgusting stomach flu. My catering license had just been suspended. Anything to get out of it.

What the heck was I trying to prove? Who the heck was I trying to prove it to?

I picked up my cell, ready to call, when a text came in from (why was I not surprised?) Aunt Phoenix.

My aunt texts rather than talk and usually sends me her "numbers" for the Jersey Pick 4, which I always forget to play and she always wins. But sometimes she sends quotes from Maya Angelou or random folks she happens to like or African proverbs, always followed by an emoji flower. It was Maya this time.

You alone are enough. You have nothing to prove to anybody.

My aunt—and Dr. Angelou—got it right. *I* was enough. I had nothing to prove to anybody. All I could do was the best I could do.

Thank you, Aunt Phoenix, I texted back.

Just do it! was her quick response, followed by a meme of Colin Kaepernick and another emoji flower.

Harley watched me with interest. "Aunt Phoenix," I said. He nodded as if he understood. He'd met my aunts, Phoenix and Celestine, over the summer. Their fascination with each other was mutual.

If he were twenty years older, he might be a good marriage prospect for you, Celestine observed. Phoenix, who disliked the very concept of marriage, had answered her suggestion with a loud Bronx cheer. I was never sure what Aunt Phoenix's reasons were for distrusting the institution, and I'd never had the nerve to ask. Just thinking about my two aunts, though, made me smile, which was obviously contagious. Harley smiled, too, but then he turned serious.

"Listen, I can pick up anything you need, carry it wherever you want me to take it, set things up, take things down. Do the heavy lifting. I've got an appointment now, but let me know tonight, okay?" He strapped on his motorcycle helmet, giving me a reassuring pat on my shoulder.

"I don't know, Harley, I . . ."

"Promise!"

I nodded that I would. Louella, quietly listening, made her offer after he'd gone. "I owe you, too, Dessa. I can help you cook if you tell me what to do, set everything up if I know where to put it. Anything you want."

"You know who this brunch is for, don't you?" I said, recalling her reaction to Osborne.

"Yeah, but we need the money, me and Red. I want Erika to go to camp later this summer, and he's doing some odd jobs—working for a landscaper, helping stack bags in a garden store, stuff like that—but nothing pays good. I don't need to tell Red everything I do, and I sure won't tell him about this. I'm probably overreacting anyway," she added, as if reminding herself of her independence. "And remember you promised to show me how to cook? I'm sick of McDonald's and Kentucky Fried Chicken. I want to feed everybody healthy stuff. This would be a chance for me to learn. All I can do right is fry bacon and scramble eggs."

I suspected she was right about the bacon and eggs, and I had promised I'd teach her how to cook. I was also glad to hear that she wanted to be more independent. From what I'd heard, Red was overly protective of both Louella and their daughter. She'd also mentioned once that he had a temper. She didn't give any details, but it still made me uncomfortable. Red didn't sound like a bad guy, and I wondered how long the two of them would be together but kept my thoughts to myself. She was still young, and it was important for her to strike out on her own as much as she could, even if it was just to prove to herself she could do it. Down the line, she might be able to help me with some catering jobs later on.

It just might work. Ordinarily I'd need two assistants for a party like this, but it was too late to hire anyone. Louella and Harley might be a good fit. Harley could do the heavy work, like he said, and Louella could help with the cooking and serving. She was a quick study, eager to learn new things, and it would be an opportunity to show her some kitchen basics. Now would be as good a time as any.

"Well?" Louella reminded me her question was hanging in the air.

"It's going to be a very busy two days. Will you have the time, with Erika?"

"I promise I won't let you down," she said with such determination that I knew she was good for her word.

I studied the photos of the living room, visualizing how I could make the space work for thirty guests and two assistants. I'd place two long buffet tables against the wall to hold the small luncheon plates. Five round tables with chairs that could seat six would be set with silverware, glassware, napkins, and an understated centerpiece. Everything would be brought and arranged the night before, like I'd told Mrs. Osborne, and I'd be there early enough on Sunday morning to do what I needed to do. The food—no nuts, no meat—needed to be dishes easy to prepare the night before and serve with minimal prep and arrangement in the morning. I'd need to do a menu I could make with my eyes closed: quiches (collard green, broccoli and cheese, mushroom), leek tarte, muffins, assorted jams, salmon croquettes—baked, not fried—small veggie platter, and sugar cookies for dessert along with coffee and assorted teas. It would be hard work, but suddenly I knew I could pull it off. Thanks to Maya Angelou, Colin Kaepernick, and . . . Aunt Phoenix.

I called the party rental place we always used and was touched by their fond memories of D&D Delights and Darryl. They were glad to know we were back in business and eager to do what they could to help. My small kitchen was soon stuffed with everything I needed to cook. My only concern was Juniper, who curiously, hungrily, longingly surveyed everything within his sight.

The rental deliveries came on Saturday, and Harley was at the Osbornes' place ready to bring them into the house through the back door and set everything up. When Louella stepped into my kitchen, she stopped short, maybe remembering the last time she'd come here. It was before the heartbreaking situation with her mother, and the night she'd shared the history that still haunted her. We sat for a while, Louella admiring again my kitchen, which is painted celestial blue and trimmed in white. "I feel like I'm in heaven," she said, and I smiled despite myself because I often felt the same way. I made a pot of rooibos tea to boost our energy, and we talked awhile about the past year. But not for long. We had work to do, and we both knew it.

We were up past midnight cooking, prepping, plating, packing everything that needed to be cooked, prepped, plated, and packed. We each toasted a job well done with a glass of merlot when the clock struck one. I baked two extra collard green quiches for myself and stuck them in the freezer for later use. You never know when you might need an extra quiche! At the last minute, I realized I'd forgotten the assorted jams for the muffins, then remembered the peach preserves Aunt Phoenix had canned over the summer. They would be a tasty, colorful addition to the marmalade and strawberry jam that happened to be in my fridge.

Louella and I were at the Osborne house early Sunday morning ready to roll. Shortly before the first guest arrived, Casey Osborne strolled in from a closed room off the kitchen, sipping what could have been bourbon, which he quickly gulped down. He filled a fancy-looking blender with almond milk, strawberries, and blueberries, then opened a large glass jar filled with what looked like seeds. He took a sniff, wrinkled his nose like a kid does when he smells something nasty, screwed it closed, and put it back on the counter. He blended the fruit mixture, poured it into two large glasses, and gulped one down. Slicing a piece of quiche, he tasted it, sprinkled it with about a teaspoon of salt, then ordered us to add more to what was left on the platter. I nodded obediently, sucking my teeth with annoyance when he left.

"She said light salt; he wants more. It's fine as is. His taste buds must be dead. Ignore him!" I muttered when Louella picked up the salt to sprinkle the dish. "Just put the shakers on the table where he can see them. If he wants to make his food inedible he can do it himself."

"You think he's going to drink both glasses of that fruity mess?" Louella asked.

"One is probably for his wife. She claims to just drink smoothies and only eat healthy."

"That look healthy to you with no veggies? Wonder what he was drinking when he came downstairs, seemed to enjoy the heck out of that." We chuckled at the thought and then at him for acting like a spoiled kid.

The afternoon sun pouring in through the windows seemed to make everything sparkle—from the shiny bone china to Osborne's phony grin. Grovesville high society (of which I am not a member) had turned out big for this afternoon event. The hum of refined chatter and mannered laughter floated through the room like incense, creating an ambiance assuring those who belonged they were welcomed and those who didn't they should get out fast. I was not surprised to see Laura Grace and Margaret Sullivan, two ladies from the Aging Readers Club, comfortably mingling with this well-heeled crowd. They were probably surprised to see me but too genteel to show it.

"You into a little bit of everything, aren't you, darling," said Laura Grace with delight, her curly, gray-speckled natural haircut a perfect match with her shiny sterling silver earrings. I had met her and the other ladies of her reading club while looking out for Harley Wilde last year. "So where's our boy? Keeping out of trouble, I hope," she added, taking a leisurely sip of her Bloody Mary.

"We sure don't need any more of that, trouble, I mean," added Margaret Sullivan, the tall graying blonde standing beside her, finishing off her champagne.

"Harley is helping me with this event," I said without going into detail.

"Keep him busy," advised Laura Grace, sounding like the retired teacher she was. "And I'll call you about our next event. I'd like you to cater it," she added, and floated away to mingle with the other guests. Things were paying off already.

Tanya Risko, chunky gold hoops an unfortunate choice in a room full of pearls, grinned and clung to Tyler Chase like a barnacle. He was handsome in what Darryl would call pretty-boy-playing-ghetto. His deep brown skin, well-shaped beard, and arched eyebrows were nicely set off by the tiny diamond stud in his right ear. The look was GQ with polish and no spit. I thought about Harley's take on him and wondered if he was right. He must have felt my eyes on him because he looked up at me, startled, and I caught a glimpse of a cloudy gray-black glimmer gone in a blink. He gave a cunning smile meant to pass as charming and glanced away.

"Do you think they saw us?" Louella asked, eyes wide and innocent, as the two passed us by with nary a nod.

"Couldn't miss," I said, placing a bowl of freshly baked muffins on the table.

"Just out the oven?" somebody asked, and I answered with an enthusiastic nod.

"That man thinks he's cute. I can tell that about him. But he has been that way since high school. I can see why he'd ignore us, but Mrs. Risko"—Louella added an exaggerated eye roll—"Mrs. Richie Rich Tanya Risko works with us every day. She could at least look in our direction." Louella, following behind me, placed a dainty cut-glass bowl of Aunt Phoenix's peach preserves next to the muffins.

"We are the help, so don't expect anyone to say much."

"I could tell you things . . ." Louella muttered.

"Don't. Just make sure you keep those platters full, the coffee hot, and that there are plenty of bottles of Fiji water. These folks are drinking liquor like it's cocktail hour at the Savoy."

Between the two of us running, fetching, pouring, grinning, the afternoon went quickly, everything going just fine . . . until it wasn't.

We were moving leftovers into the kitchen and sugar cookies next to the coffee when Mona Osborne appeared. Willowy and elegant, she floated down the stairs and into the living room. Men and women alike took a collective breath as she made her dramatic entrance. I recalled her words about showing up in her pretty little dress with her pretty little smile; she was clearly a woman of her word. The dress was silk, pink and clingy, highlighting her caramel-colored skin and pregnant belly. Her hair, long and thick, was piled on top of her head, tendrils drifting down to her perfectly oval face. She gazed around the room for a moment, gracing her guests with a wide "pretty little smile," then headed for Tanya and Tyler. Tanya all but genuflected when she approached, for which she received a brush of a kiss. Tyler, on the other hand, got a lingering hug when he gently patted Mona's belly. Did anyone besides me notice their quick, passing intimacy?

Apparently, somebody else did, and that was Casey Osborne. He stood stiff and stern across the room, gobbling down a muffin so quickly I thought he might choke. He studied the three of them like a bird of prey, then slowly swooped toward them, taking his own good time. But then abruptly he turned as if he'd picked up the scent of a fresher, more vulnerable creature. He headed to the bar and the untidy woman and the boy who stood beside her.

Aurelia Osborne was only a few years older than me but had the sagging face and cross expression of a woman who long ago forgot how to smile. Her loosely fitting pewter-gray dress with the kind of shoulder pads that died in the eighties was better suited for a wake than brunch; she brought to mind a pigeon lost in a room of cardinals. I studied her carefully, looking for a hint of glimmer, but saw nothing except gray, which cast her in shadow, much like the one that once shadowed Vinton. She must have sensed my attention, because she immediately turned in my direction.

"Odessa! Odessa Jones! What are you doing here?" she yelled.

The room filled with polite tittering grew silent as people watched her clumsily make her way across the floor toward me. Her son, Lacey, followed behind, head buried in his chest. I managed a quick glance at Casey Osborne, whose face was taut with anger as he came toward us.

"Aurelia, how are you? I'm so glad to see you, but I'm working. I can't talk," I whispered.

"I haven't seen you in years. Not in years!" she said, her voice growing louder as she weaved back and forth, bumping into me and then Lacey, whose eyes were nearly closed like they'd been in that photograph I'd first seen of him. "This spinach or whatever quiche is to die for. Promise me we'll get together so we can catch up. Promise me, promise me!" she said, like an impatient child. "I don't have anything to write on. Can you give me two of your cards and I can write down my number on one?"

"Sure." I handed her several cards from my apron pocket.

She scribbled down both her cell and landline number as well as her address and gave one back. I quickly stuffed it into my pocket.

"Do you promise to call me?" she asked again.

"I promise." I noticed a bit of collard green leaf had lodged itself on a front tooth. I moved toward her to let her know, but it was too late; Casey Osborne was upon us.

"Go home, you drunken fool. Can't you see you're humiliating the boy. Lacey, come with me. It was good to see you yesterday, Son. Thanks for thinking about me, for bringing me that flax. I got my next move figured out, too," he said with a chuckle. Pushing me out of the way, Osborne grabbed his son by one arm just as Aurelia grabbed him by the other in what quickly became a parental tug-of-war. Several guests surreptitiously made their way toward us, eager for post-brunch gossip. Embarrassed, I gazed at the floor.

"I want to go with my dad! Let me go, Mom, please. I need to be with my dad!" Lacey finally pulled away from his mother, whose expression of loathing toward her ex-husband distorted her face. Reluctantly, she let the boy go, dropping her hands to her sides.

"You'll get what's coming to you, you son of a bitch, and I'll be damned if you'll get my child!" she said to Osborne, her voice hoarse with anger. "And your tramp of a wife will get what she deserves, too. I'll have the last laugh on both of you, I promise you that, sure as I breathe," she added, at which several guests standing nearby audibly gasped.

A sudden crash like an omen followed her words as loud voices coming from the kitchen drew my and Osborne's attention. I desperately searched for Louella, who was nowhere to be found. There was another bang, and I dashed in the direction of the noise, followed by Osborne, who pushed me out of the way as he burst through the swinging door into the kitchen.

Once upon a time, I would gladly have lived in this space,

to say nothing of cooking in it. It was stylishly done up like the rest of the house, mostly in white and gray and stainless-steel appliances that gleamed like new. The granite counters looked as if they'd been just been washed, and ceiling lights, twinkling like tiny stars, dotted the ceiling—but all that had changed. The gleaming lights now shone down mercilessly on the hodgepodge of food and liquids that covered the newly polished wood floor. Mashed salmon cakes, squashed quiche, dripping dip, formed a disgusting, slippery mess wherever you stepped. In the middle of it all was Harley Wilde, dressed in black, pinning a bear of a man down on the floor.

I'd never seen Red Bailey before, so it took me a minute to realize that this man must be the "gentle giant" Louella so often described. He was big and burly, built like a linebacker, yet with Erika's reddish coloring and light eyes, which softened his look. But there was no gentleness about him now. He was grunting and flailing his arms as he desperately tried to shake loose from Harley's hold. Louella knelt on the messy floor beside them, sobbing and stroking Red's face.

"I'm so sorry, baby. I shouldn't have come. I know I shouldn't have come," she wept into his ear.

"What the hell are you doing back in my house? Didn't I tell you to stay away from me? Who the hell let you in here?" Osborne screamed, heading toward Red and Harley.

"Mr. Osborne, I'm so sorry," I muttered, as baffled as he was. "I'm not sure what is going on here, but I will find out. This is Louella, my assistant, I introduced you earlier, and—"

Before I could finish, Red picked his head up from the floor and tried to spit in Osborne's face. "You ain't nothing but a damn thief. I told you that before!" His face, red and contorted with rage, was earning him his nickname. "Harley, you know what he did to my family, man; you better get off me before I get loose, or I'll take you out, too. He'll get what he has coming. I swore that on my daddy's grave."

"I told you before to stay the hell away from me and my family!" Osborne said, evenly and spiteful. "I told you to talk to my lawyers about what you think I owe you. I told you before about breaking into my house."

What the heck was he talking about? "He's been here before?" I asked in bewilderment. Nobody seemed to hear me.

"He doesn't mean any harm; he doesn't know what he's saying. He had to be here on your property, that was his job. He just came here today to see me. He didn't know you lived here!" cried Louella, pleading for Osborne's understanding from her spot on the floor.

"Shut up, you cheap little whore! I know who and what you are." Osborne turned his anger toward Louella, who ducked away from him as if his words were blows.

"Man, I'll kill you for that! Just like I kill your damn rats. You'll die just like them rats do, rolling and screaming on the ground, because that's what you are, a filthy rat!" said Red, who had managed to pry himself from Harley's grip and was now standing up.

"Rats! You have rats!" I squealed in horror.

"Man, you ain't killing nobody today." Harley grabbed Red again, holding him tightly. Louella jumped up off the floor and ran to assist him, and somehow the two of them shoved and pushed Red against the wall and finally out the back door into the driveway. I heard him screaming and cursing on the way out as he slammed somebody's car with his fist.

Osborne and I stood silent in the chaos that surrounded us. I, resorting to the default role of responsible caterer, began cleaning up the kitchen, bending, scrubbing, and avoiding Osborne's eyes as I wiped up what I could with whatever I could find. Osborne grabbed me by the shoulders, forcing me to look at him.

"You ain't getting a red cent for this, not as long as I'm alive. When I'm through with you—"

"Let her go," Harley said, stepping back into the kitchen from outside. "She didn't have nothing to do with this mess. Take your hands off her!"

"I'm so sorry about this, Mr. Osborne," I stammered, begging as hard as I could. "I'll take care of everything. I'm so sorry!"

I'd always heard the Hand of Death grabs you when you least expect it, when The Reaper, as Aunt Phoenix calls him, is turning in your number. But my number wasn't up today, and there were *two* hands on my shoulders, squeezing me so tightly I could feel each finger dig deep into my flesh. No color was in Osborne's face. His eyes were slits; his lips stretched across his teeth in a grimace of pain. He let me go then, his hands falling to his sides.

"Mr. Osborne?" His eyes grew wide, as if he was surprised by the sound of my voice, then he staggered backwards, dropping at my feet. Harley and I glanced at each other and at the man writhing on the floor beneath us. When he stopped moving, Harley knelt beside him, searched for a pulse, then glanced up at me.

"He's dead, Dessa!" he said as if he couldn't believe his own words.

Chapter 3

The brunch cleared out fast; sudden death has a way of doing that. Even the corpse was gone—carried away by two muscular ambulance attendants with downcast eyes and somber bearings. Mona Osborne and Tyler Chase came into the kitchen claiming to look for Osborne shortly after he dropped dead. They gasped in unison, glared at me and Harley for a minute, quickly glanced at each other, and Chase promptly called the police. When the cops came, Mona clasped her belly, moaned, and told Detective Ramos, the man in charge, that she felt faint. Ramos was an older man, short, plump, with an abundance of curly gray hair, who looked like he'd walked the streets more times than he cared to remember and was eagerly waiting for retirement. I suspected this was supposed to be an easy beat and unexpected death wasn't supposed to be part of it.

Ramos gave Mona a sympathetic pat on her shoulder, suggested she call her doctor, and advised that she "take to her bed," as he put it. Chase pulled the detective aside, whispered a few words to him after giving him his card, then promptly left the kitchen, leaving me and Harley, hunched together like two guilty kids, at the scene of a crime, which wasn't yet a crime—but might be—according to Ramos. I was relieved he wasn't one of those who had interviewed me and my co-workers after the demise of my former boss last year. Thank God for tender mercies.

Apparently, Harley wasn't sure those mercies extended to him. He looked worried and scared, two things you definitely don't want to be in front of cops, especially if you're black. Luckily, the officer addressed his first question to me.

"I'm Detective Ramos. I'll need your names, addresses, your business here, and I'd like to know what happened this afternoon." Ramos looked like he might be about the same age as Osborne. I wondered if he'd grown up in Grovesville and knew him. Ramos might have been one of the adoring fans shouting from the grandstands who cheered "Case" on in those old glory days. His expression, however, revealed nothing but a passive interest in what had just happened. Even though I tried to be calm, I haltingly delivered my first answers, with so many *um*s and *ah*s while nervously fingering my mother's talisman, the man probably assumed I was lying.

"Well, um, the brunch was over and ah, ah, me and, uh, my assistant were bringing plates in from the living room, and uh, we heard something fall, and found that some things had fallen on the floor and then Mr. Osborne came in to check and . . . uh, seemed to have a heart attack!"

Eyes wide, breath catching in my throat, I hoped that covered it all. It didn't.

"So, you are the caterer, and you're telling me that you and your assistant were cleaning up after this party and the deceased came in to check on you and dropped dead?" Ramos stared at me with what might be called a jaundiced eye before he continued.

"Let me see if I've got this right, Mrs. Jones. So this gentleman, all in black, your catering assistant, was helping you bring in the platters when you heard a crash, came into the kitchen, found something had fallen, which I guess explains this mess, and then the deceased came in and fell dead at your feet."

Harley, standing beside me, stiffened. Well aware of the dangers of lying to the police, he blurted out the truth—some of it anyway.

"I was here in the kitchen to help Mrs. Jones clean up after the party and make sure the rentals were returned. She and Mr. Osborne came into the kitchen to check on a noise they heard, and then he died."

"Then he died?"

"Yes, sir. Then he died."

"What was the noise that brought you both in here?" Ramos turned back to me. Harley answered.

"Someone who wasn't supposed to be here was in the kitchen, and I was trying to get him out. We fell on the floor when I tried to get him out. Mr. Osborne came into the kitchen when he heard the noise and ordered the man to leave, and I was able to get him out," Harley said, running his words together in a long, leaky spiel.

Studying Harley as if he were speaking in tongues, Ramos then turned to me. "So what happened to this . . . intruder?"

"He left," Harley said.

"How did he leave?"

"He and his fiancée got into their car and drove home," I chimed in.

"So the intruder's fiancée was here with him? They both broke in here together. Did they know the deceased, Mr. Osborne? Why were they both here? Did they have something to do with his death? Most importantly, who were they?" The questions came like spitfire. I had the uncomfortable feeling that Harley and I had entered the realm of suspects.

Lucky for me, we were saved by my trusty rental agency crew, who noisily piled into the kitchen. The owner glanced at the detective, then gave me a nod, and his crew made quick, efficient work of transporting and removing all their rentals. He wasn't sure what was going on but had the good sense not to be any part of it. I quickly and wordlessly wrote him a check for what was owed, praying it wouldn't bounce but knowing it had nearly emptied my checking account. Osborne had vowed I wouldn't get a red cent as long as he was alive. That was now the bitter truth.

Detective Ramos, sitting on the edge of a stool at the counter, observed the unfolding activity, waiting patiently for the rental people to finish. It was clear he wasn't finished with the two of us. Suddenly he stood up and walked around the kitchen, stepped into the living room and back, as if counting steps, then peeked into the small room from where Osborne had come before the brunch began. He stepped inside, lingering for a moment before coming out.

"This room looks like a study. Fancy chessboard set up on his desk. White queen ready to be taken by black's knight. Wonder who he was playing with? Wife, business partner? Strange place to put a study, so close to the kitchen. Do you all know what he used this room for besides playing chess?"

Ramos seemed to be talking more to himself than to me and Harley, but we shook our heads simultaneously, as if attached by a string. He stepped back into the kitchen and sat down at the counter to confront us again.

"None of this is making sense to me, so I'm going to ask you two again. I want to hear some answers this time. All of them. As far as I can see, this looks like a case of accidental death, an older guy having a sudden heart attack, but I can't be sure of that until I hear from the ME. What I do know, is if I don't hear something that sounds like the truth, you both risk becoming suspects. Do you understand that, or do you want to go down to the station?"

We shook our heads in unison again, puppets still on a string.

"Who was the intruder and who is his fiancée?"

"A man named Avon Bailey Jr., who goes by 'Red.' His fiancée is Louella Jefferson," Harley said.

"And your name again?"

"Harley Wilde."

Ramos's eyes narrowed for an instant, which told me he'd heard one or all of the names before.

"Is she the daughter of the woman we arrested for a double murder here in town last year?" he asked, turning to me.

There was no sense in giving the man more than he already knew, so I ducked part of his question. "Louella Jefferson is my assistant. She works with me at . . ." I paused for a tortuous moment. "Risko Realty."

"Risko Realty!" Despite his best effort to conceal it, Ramos couldn't hide his amusement. Risko Realty must have become a running macabre joke down at the station. Harley Wilde, Louella Jefferson. Avon Bailey. Apparently, Ramos had heard the names before. He turned to me as if I might be a bearer of truth.

"Let's have it again," he said, his eyes narrowing. Harley, grateful not to have been asked and wary of saying anything more, stared at the floor.

Somehow, I managed to get it all out. "Louella and I were bringing things into the kitchen. I went back into the living room. I heard a crash. I came back and found Mr. Wilde trying to get Red, Mr. Bailey, out of the kitchen. Mr. Wilde was here to help me clean up and prepare for the rentals. Mr. Osborne followed me in here, had a few words with Mr. Bailey. Then Mr. Wilde and Louella took him outside to his car and Mr. Wilde came back inside to finish helping and that was when Mr. Osborne died."

"Just like that?"

"Just like that," I answered, hoping I sounded sure of myself.

"What did Bailey, this so-called Red, say to the deceased?"

"He accused him of being a thief," said Harley. "Called him a rat."

"Did Osborne steal something from him? Never mind. We'll get to the bottom of things on our own," Ramos said, answering the question for himself. "So who called the police?"

"Tyler Chase," Harley and I said in unison.

"His business partner," I added.

"He didn't stick around long," Ramos said more to himself. He scribbled something on his pad, then turned back to us.

"One more question, then I'll let you two finish what you came here to do,'" he said, with a critical glance at the mess on the floor and leftovers on the platters. "You're the caterer, right. What's the name of your company?"

"D&D Delights."

"Do you have a catering license?"

"Yes," I said, hoping with a sudden pang in my stomach that I'd remembered to renew it.

"What was your menu? What did you serve?"

The question took me by surprise. For one awkward moment, I thought he was considering hiring me. "Well, I—"

"Was anything home canned?" he impatiently interrupted. "Like, say, jellies, pickles, food that could harbor botulism?"

The air went out of me. "Well, I served some peach preserves that my aunt canned last year, but I—"

There was no need to say more; he cut me off again. "That your aunt canned last year? How old is your aunt? Would you say she is elderly?"

"Yes, I guess you could say that, but—"

"Give me a sample so I can have it tested, then pass it on to the medical examiner."

Fearfully and dutifully, I collected Aunt Phoenix's home-canned preserves and gave it to the detective. "I don't think—"

"Don't serve this or cater anything else until you hear from me or the medical examiner, do you understand? We need to establish that this or something else you served was not the source of Mr. Osborne's demise." Ramos closed his notebook, surveyed the scene once more, then looked the two of us over one last time. "This isn't a crime scene . . . yet, but it may be. The medical examiner will get back to you, Mrs. Caterer, as soon as he tests this jelly. The two of you will hear from me or another officer shortly. Do you understand?"

With a dismissive headshake, he didn't wait for an answer. Neither of us spoke as we obediently cleaned up the mess, collected our belongings, and left the scene of . . . whatever.

Harley followed me home on his bike, more because he needed to talk than out of concern for my personal safety. It was clear that we both needed something more than herbal tea to calm us down, so I dug out the bottle of brandy that I reserve for flambés. The rule for liquor in food—be it wine or spirits—is to use the best, and, thankfully, this was a good one. I filled two snifters and we settled down next to each other on the couch and sipped in silence. Juniper, my Temptations-begging cat, broke the quiet by jumping into Harley's lap and mewing for treats.

Harley grinned. "Wow, I've never had a cat take to me like this," he said, genuinely flattered. "He must know I'm connected to Parker. They must have hung out together when he was staying with you last year."

"Maybe so," I said, noncommittal. I had "watched" Parker, Harley's pet parakeet, when he'd spent some time in jail last year for a crime of which he was innocent. I didn't have the heart to tell him that Juniper had jumped in his lap because he was sitting in Juniper's spot. Parker, Harley's noisy little bird, had barely escaped Juniper's eager claws. As Aunt

Phoenix had reminded me at the time . . . cats will be cats and birds will be birds, which had been the truth.

"Oh Lord, help me," I said aloud at the thought of Aunt Phoenix and her preserves.

"Yeah," said Harley; assuming my sigh was about this afternoon, he shook his head in agreement. I took a gulp of brandy, enjoying the strength of the liquor as it traveled down my throat, going straight to my head. "Man, that dude just showed up out of nowhere. He broke into that house like he'd been there before. Said he had a beef with Osborne about what happened to his family, but that was a long time ago, Dessa. And we all were involved in that mess. That stuff with Charlie Risko. You know what I'm talking about."

I didn't comment because it was before my time, but I knew only too well.

"I knew there was going to be trouble, so I was trying to get him out, but all he wanted to do was fight. He can be a nice guy, but he's always had a temper."

"And he'd been at the house before?"

Harley waited a minute before answering, then shrugged as if he didn't want to say it. "That's what the man said."

I let his answer that wasn't one slide without saying anything as I watched him sip his brandy. "I asked Louella about going over there, and if Red would be on her case about it, but she said she needed the money, so I took her at her word."

"Mistake number one," he said quietly and without blame. "Dessa, I can't have the cops sniffing around my life another time. I can't go through *that* again. I'm just grateful he wasn't one of the guys who arrested me the last time."

"You don't need to worry. At least there was no smoking gun." I hadn't meant it as a joke, but he laughed—gallows humor, they call it—and I joined in.

"I wonder what they're going to ask Louella and Red? You know they're going to talk to them. Red might have a record, and you know Louella . . ." He paused because we both knew about her past and neither of us wanted to dwell on it.

"Osborne probably just died of a heart attack. He didn't look all that healthy to me and he was drinking something hard when he came into the kitchen," I said as if saying it would make it so.

"Yeah, that's what it was," Harley quickly agreed, and took another sip of brandy. "He looked kind of bad when he came into the office. You never know what's going to take out a guy his age."

I nodded vigorously; yet another possibility had crossed my mind, and no matter how hard I shook and how much brandy I sipped (and it was a lot), those what-ifs were looming large. What if Aunt Phoenix hadn't preserved those peaches correctly? She was getting older; maybe she'd done something wrong, added the wrong ingredient, didn't cook them long enough. What if they killed Osborne and he'd died of botulism from something that I gave him?

Involuntary manslaughter lodged itself in my brain. Whatever the ME found out, this could be the end of D&D Delights, to say nothing of me. Who would be foolish enough to hire me after something like this?

"I better be on my way," Harley said, standing up and bringing my thoughts back to him.

"You okay to ride?"

"I been drunker than this." He chuckled, then paused, not hiding his concern. "Don't worry, Dessa, stuff is going to work out. It always does."

My smile was feeble, my heart and mind not in it.

"Do you think I should call Louella and warn her the cops might call her about Red?"

"I think you should say as little about this to anybody, especially them. We didn't know that Red was going to freak out like he did. Truth be told, they weren't there when Osborne died. It was just us."

"Yeah, our bad luck."

It was late by the time Harley left, but there was one call I had to make before going to bed. I wasn't looking forward to it.

Aunt Phoenix, unlike many people her age (and nobody, including me, was sure exactly what that was), stayed up late after always enjoying a daily siesta, reminding anybody who dared to ask that no red meat, lots of olive oil, and cherry brandy were the keys to aging well with all your wits. Darryl made the mistake of reminding her that daily naps were usually taken in places hotter than Jersey, to which she snapped that it was hot *somewhere* in the world and to mind his own business. He'd nodded in agreement and wisely left it alone.

The preserves had been canned last summer. Canned goods were safe for a year, but had she remembered to store them in a cool, dark place? Were the lids new? She was notoriously thrifty. Had she bought new jars? Had she forgotten to do something? I turned on my iPhone and asked Siri the symptoms for botulism: "Blurred vision, droopy eyelids, slurred speech, muscle weakness." Osborne had looked bad; could botulism be the source?

Knowing Aunt Phoenix's preference for text over talk, I sent her a question:

Just curious. Have you eaten any of those delicious peach preserves you canned last summer?

Her response was immediate.

Huh?

I picked up the phone and FaceTimed her—hoping she would accept the call. I needed to make sure she didn't take out her hearing aid, her usual ploy when she wants to avoid talking to you.

"This must be important for you to want to see my face

this late at night," she said, her voice gruffer than usual. "What's this mess about my peach preserves?"

"Hi, Aunt Phoenix, glad to see you're still up," I said, neutrally.

"What's up?"

"Well—"

"I was doing preserves before you were born," she reminded me before I could answer.

"I know, but there's been some question—"

"I had some for breakfast yesterday morning. What's the question?"

"Well, um . . ."

"You can ask your aunt Celestine about my preserves. She took some back with her, but she's liable to say there's some problem just to spite me. I was always better at canning than her. Ever since we were girls."

"Aunt Phoenix, do you know what botulism is?" I got right to the point, regretting the words the moment I said them.

"Of course I know what botulism is. What do you take me for, an old fool? Anyone who doesn't know how to can properly isn't worth her canning jars."

"Please don't be defensive," I pleaded, a cowed child.

"I'm not being defensive," she snapped defensively, then added, "Did somebody have a problem with my preserves?" She sounded worried and, much worse, scared, and began to speak more to herself than to me. "Maybe I made a mistake. Maybe I'm just not up to canning anymore, maybe—"

I winced at the rare sound of self-defeat in her voice. "Stop it, Aunt Phoe," I said, calling her by the nickname I used when I was a kid. "You're fine. The preserves are fine. They're delicious. I served some today and everybody loved them. It's just late and I've had too much brandy and—I wanted to hear your voice because I was lonely," I added a quick, covering lie.

"If you sipped brandy during the day, it wouldn't affect you in the evening," she said, back to her old self. "I love you, too, Odessa," she added, anticipating as always what I was going to say before hanging up.

"I love you, too," I said, turning off the phone, finishing off what was left of the brandy, and giving Juniper the Temptations he'd been whining for since Harley left. There was no sense talking about bad preserves, botulism, and worrying my aunt until I knew something definite. I'd figure out then the best way to handle it. The question was, when would that answer come?

Chapter 4

Detective Ramos called Tuesday morning to tell me that Aunt Phoenix's preserves had passed whatever test was given and hadn't caused Casey Osborne's death. They suspected he'd been poisoned but weren't sure how or by whom. The Osborne kitchen had been designated a crime scene, he added, so Harley and I were considered material witnesses. Ramos warned me not to leave town or talk to anybody about what had happened and to expect to be interviewed in more detail at a later date. The good news: Aunt Phoenix's peach preserves didn't kill somebody. The bad news: Being a material witness sounded almost as bad as being a suspect.

By that afternoon, everybody in town knew about the local millionaire's suspicious death. They also knew a small firm named D&D Delights had catered the fatal party. Needless to say, Aunt Phoenix called before the day was done.

"You mean to tell me you didn't get some kind of warning?" she asked in disbelief.

"No, and don't mention our worthless gift again. Aunt Phoenix, are you still there?" I asked after what seemed two minutes. She'd taken so long to answer I thought she'd hung up.

"What can I do?" she asked, her tone gentler.

"Can you burn something?" I asked, only half joking.

"I'll check with Celestine and get back to you," she said, taking me seriously. "In the meantime, sharpen your skills, notice the signs, use your nose, and above all watch for glimmers. They will tell you what you need to know if you pay attention."

I assumed because we were on the phone she couldn't see my eyes roll. Fool, me!

"Odessa, listen!" she said with a snap I hadn't heard in years.

"I will," I said, the chastised child. When she hung up I turned off my phones—landline and cell—and crawled into bed with a blanket over my head to wait for Wednesday morning. I hadn't heard from Harley. I'd called him twice after speaking to Ramos and he hadn't answered, which meant Ramos had talked to him, too. I knew I had to go back to Risko Realty sooner or later, but I didn't want to see anyone, especially Louella. I'd given the cops her phone number and address. I hadn't had much choice but felt guilty anyway, as if I'd betrayed her. I had no idea how Tanya would feel about the death of her friend and possible business partner. As for Vinton, I simply didn't want to hear his mouth.

I came in early, grateful there was nobody there—at least in corporeal form. More often than not, I could sense the presence of those who had died violent deaths here—the murdered Charlie Risko; his brother Stuart, who had taken his own life. I knew their anguished spirits were still hanging around, lonely and defiant.

"Good morning, you-all," I said, thankful that nobody answered. I checked my e-mail, deleting those whose senders I didn't recognize, then went through the listings to see if there was anything new. I was working with four clients, two looking for apartments, two for starter homes. When I found some possibilities, I attached the files and e-mailed them. I didn't want to chance somebody asking about Sunday.

Five e-mails, though, lightened my heart. Three were from Lennox Royal, owner of Royal's Regal Barbecue, one from Laura Grace of the Aging Readers Club, and another from Julie Russell, my next-door neighbor. Without mentioning the obvious, all asked how I was doing and requested my services. Lennox wanted to know if I could drop off three cakes and a pie when I got a chance. Laura reminded me I'd promised to cater her Aging Readers Club luncheon and wanted to meet soon so we could discuss a menu, and Julie, bless her heart, invited me to dinner but only if I brought dessert. Each was letting me know they believed in me and trusted my cooking, and all lifted my spirits. They went even higher when Harley sauntered into the office carrying his motorcycle helmet in one hand and my latte grande in the other.

"Anybody here?" He glanced nervously around the room, lingering for an instant on Tanya's closed door.

"Just us spirits," I said. He jumped, then scowled, which made me chuckle. "You're early this morning. You don't usually show up till noon."

"I was sick of being home, and I don't appreciate that crack about us spirits, Dessa, that ain't even funny. This place must be haunted. Seems like something bad happens around here every time you turn around."

"Well, Osborne did die in his house," I said, trying to reassure Harley, but I fingered my mother's talisman just in case.

He sat a few chairs down from me, turned on his laptop, and opened his coffee. "Ever since Stuart died, seems like there's some kind of curse on this place."

"It's coincidence," I said lightly, but made a mental note to ask Aunt Phoenix how to get rid of wounded spirits. I'd burned some sage one night after everybody had left but obviously needed something stronger. "Did the cops talk to you yet?" I said, eager to change a subject I was too well acquainted with.

"They're going to interview me again, told me not to talk to anybody about what happened. Guess it's okay to talk to you, though. I sure don't want any more trouble with cops."

"I won't tell if you don't," I said. "Did you know that Red had been there before?"

Harley shook his head. "Not until Osborne said it. I think he must have been talking about the yard. They probably have storage sheds or a pool house or something like that outside. Looked like at least an acre; most big places like that do."

We sat with our thoughts for a while, Harley probably dreading his interview with the cops, me worried about Louella. I wondered, too, about Red, and his influence. Many a good woman has been dragged down by the likes of a bad man. Time would tell if he was really bad or just had bad luck. Then I started thinking about Bertie, Louella's mother, wondering if legacies can be passed down through families. Almost like the gift. Although I never promised to look out for what Bertie once considered her "wayward" daughter, I knew she'd expect it of me. *You're my mother's only friend,* Louella had told me the night before both their worlds came crashing down, and that had been the truth.

Harley and I both glanced at the door. The sharp, acrid scent of bitter lemon caught our attention, marking the arrival of Vinton Laverne. Harley slipped in his ear buds. I steeled myself for Vinton's mouth. Ignoring Harley, he settled down next to me, grabbed my hands, and gently squeezed them before letting them go.

"What the hell happened?" he asked.

"Hell!" I said, uttering the simple truth.

Slowly and deliberately he shook his head. "Sunshine, I knew that man was trouble the minute he walked into this office. Knew it!"

"Didn't you want to help out at the bar? Make some of your killer martinis." Hindsight, for Vinton as for most folks, was twenty-twenty.

"Seems like there was enough dying going on over there without my killer martinis," he said, as fast on his feet as he used to be with Bertie, which made me think about her again and then about Louella. They must have come to his mind, too. "Have you talked to Louella? She didn't come in yesterday either. They don't think she had anything to do with him dying, do they? The news said his death was suspicious."

"I don't think so," I said, praying that they didn't. "Red showed up there right before the man died. They think it was a heart attack, but they don't know."

"What do you mean he showed up before he died? What happened?"

"Keep your mouth closed, Dessa. Remember what the cop said," Harley warned, having taken out his ear buds.

Vinton moved closer. "So what did the cop say?"

"Mind your business, old man," Harley teased as he put his ear buds back in.

"He didn't say much," I said, which was the truth; Harley and I had done all the talking.

"So it was a heart attack?" Vinton asked, still fishing.

"They don't know," I said, abruptly turning back to my laptop.

"Well, I'll find out from somebody sooner or later," said Vinton, cutting bait just as Tanya breezed into the room, closing the door behind her. And she did breeze in, floating into the office as if she had nothing on her mind, with scarcely a nod at any of us.

"Ah, the queen arrives, untouched and untouchable," Vinton said in a low, catty whisper, but I knew better. Tanya was neither untouched nor untouchable.

To those without the gift or keen observation skills, Tanya

did seem to dance through the world without missing a beat. Both her husband and lover had been brutally murdered last year, something that would destroy most women for a lifetime, but she had climbed back in life's saddle richer, prettier, and more ambitious than ever. She had few, if any, girlfriends and those who occasionally dropped by for lunch were gone within two months. The same applied to the men who came and went, which made me wonder about this new one, Tyler Chase, and what kind of shelf life he'd have.

But I knew Tanya was more than she seemed. She had shared bits and pieces about her past and the wounds that haunted her and I knew that wounds like hers were easy to conceal but never disappeared. She had no glimmer at all, but that didn't necessarily mean anything; yet it could, which made me wary. I hoped that long-handled spoon I "stirred" her with was long enough to keep me from getting burned.

Our relationship was an uneven one. When she felt lonely, she'd call me into her office as if we were best friends, giggling or weeping until she felt better, and then dismissing me with a disarming smile. I was often tempted to avoid or ignore her, but part of me (maybe my mother's grace) prevented me from cutting her off altogether. Truth was, I felt sorry for her because she was so young and had been through some bad times, so I tried to keep an ear open for listening and a place for her in my heart. She was also my boss, such as it was, and with jobs scarce these days, it would do no good to obviously snub her. So I was always there for her when she needed to talk, listened as well as I could, and offered advice that I thought might do her some good, which she rarely took.

She usually summoned me with a text (one of the only things she and Aunt Phoenix had in common). I wasn't surprised when one appeared on my phone after she'd closed her door.

"It's either Aunt P or Queen T," said Vinton, who never

missed a thing. "If it's Tanya, ask her if she's heard from Louella. I miss my Baby Doll." Although he and her mother used to bicker more than talk, he had appointed himself one of Louella's unofficial guardians.

I stepped into Tanya's office and was momentarily overwhelmed by the smell of honeysuckle from a flickering yellow candle on her desk.

"It comforts me," she said, noting my reaction as I sat down on her paisley-covered sofa. "It reminds me of good times, when things were better. Have you heard from Louella?" she asked, as if she was part of the good times. "I tried to call her to let her know I was worried about her, but she didn't answer. But I knew she was there. I could always sense that about her, even when we were kids. I know she's scared now. I would be."

"Why would you be?" I asked, genuinely curious.

"First of all, thanks for stopping in to see me," she said, changing the subject. "I have something important I want to ask you."

"Okay," I said, hesitant and doubtful.

"That was something about Casey Osborne, wasn't it?" she said, returning to the fatal brunch with surprising levity. "Tell me what really happened in that kitchen?" Her gaze focused on me as if it could dislodge some secret truth where others had failed.

"He just died, Tanya. He had a heart attack and died."

"That's not what I heard."

"You and his wife are good friends. Did she tell you something else?"

"I'm not at liberty to say," she said, cagily. "But I got the feeling it wasn't a heart attack. That it was more serious than that."

"I don't know," I said with what I hoped was a convincing shrug.

"I heard Avon Bailey was there when he died. Louella calls him Red, but I knew him from the old days. Do you know what he was doing there? I don't trust him, do you?"

"I don't really know him," I said, which was the truth.

"Just for your information, me and Mona aren't all that good friends," she added, taking a turn in a new direction. "Tyler Chase is my good friend, not her. He was really broken up about his partner's death. Tyler is a very caring man, a good man. I'll just be dealing with Tyler now with the business stuff we had planned. 'Tanya and Tyler,' that sounds good together, doesn't it?"

I nodded, obediently.

She changed directions again. "First of all, Dessa, I'm really sorry about what happened, whatever it was, and I know it wasn't your fault."

"Thanks."

"I feel like it's my fault, kind of, because I got you into it and everything. I know Mona is tight with her money, and she can be mean and probably won't want to pay you, so I want to cover what they owe you. If that's okay."

Her offer surprised and touched me. The Osborne deposit had been quickly spent on rentals and preparation and totally wiped me out. I could probably sue Mona for what was owed, but under the circumstances it would be a dumb move to make. D&D Delights didn't need more bad publicity. I hated going to Aunt Phoenix yet again for another loan, but the way things were going, I wouldn't have a choice. "Tanya, I . . ." My voice cracked, and I felt my eyes water in gratitude.

"Just say thank you, that's enough," she said, somewhat brusquely. "Just send me the bill you were going to send them and I'll cover it, okay?"

"Thank you."

"But I do have a personal favor to ask," she said after a beat.

I drew back, suspicious. Last time I did Tanya a personal favor a man dropped dead at my feet.

"Sure, whatever you need," I said, despite my doubts.

"I want to have a surprise dinner for Tyler, you know, a romantic surprise dinner that will cheer him up, help him forget about what happened. I want you to help me with it, like cater it, like *really* romantic with candles and soft music," she said breathlessly, leaning back in her chair and closing her eyes as if imagining the whole scene. She had slipped into the Tanya I'd seen at our first meeting—a wounded girl-child who believed in fantasies. "I'll light candles and play soft music and we'll sit on the floor on a blanket and have a picnic. Like a picnic," she added, smiling at her own thoughts.

"You sure you want it to be a surprise?" I asked gently. "Why don't you just invite him to dinner?"

"No, that won't work," she said, a little girl determined to have her own way. "I want it to be a surprise. He gave me the keys to his place after what happened on Sunday. I could see how upset he was and he told me to meet him there because he didn't want to be alone. He didn't ask for the keys back. That must have been his way of letting me into his life without needing to say it."

I paused a moment. "Maybe he just forgot."

"No!" she said sharply, then softened her voice, adding with a catty touch, "I think I know men better than you do, Mrs. Dessa Jones!"

"No doubt you do," I said, and left it at that. "But I do have one piece of advice. If you want a romantic dinner, don't sit on the floor. Exactly what do you want me to do? Do you want me to cook, to serve?"

She looked perplexed, and I added, "Do you want me to stay and serve?"—something I wasn't looking forward to.

"No, I want the dinner to be a surprise when we get there."

"Maybe I can cook the meal and set up his kitchen or dining room table before you come."

She thought about it for a minute. "Then you would leave?"

"If that works for you."

"Can you make it nice with classy linens and good china and crystal glasses and stuff, like they had at that brunch?"

"I'll take care of it," I said, grateful I'd paid off my rental guys and glad she'd taken my suggestion.

"What about candles? Can you have the candles lit when we come in?"

"No, Tanya. That would be a fire hazard. You can light them when the two of you come home. I'll prepare the food and you can put it in the microwave. I'll have the table set and chill the champagne before I leave."

She smiled more to herself than to me. "Get the best, okay, and good champagne, good wine. He's a real gentleman; he knows the difference."

"Of course," I said.

"I don't care about the money," she said, giving me an uncomfortable flashback to my last conversation with Mona Osborne.

"I'll come up with a menu as soon as I get back to my desk and text it to you."

"And don't use any onions or garlic or stuff that will make your breath stink or give you gas."

I nodded that I understood.

"And dessert," she said, with another dreamy look. "I want dessert."

"How about that chocolate cake I made for you before?"

She wrinkled her nose and shook her head vigorously. "No! That will bring back bad memories. Something light and sweet and pretty."

"Chocolate mousse?"

"Doesn't that go in your hair?" she asked skeptically.

"No. It's like a pudding, only . . . sexier and edible," I said without cracking a smile.

"And cognac. I want to get us both good and drunk. And some whipped cream in the refrigerator, that we can have fun with!"

I nodded without comment. "I'll come up with something good," I said, even though I had my doubts about Tanya's plans, but it was good to be back in business, and I had her to thank for that. "When do you want me to set up the dinner?"

"Saturday night. He said he'll be busy that day and I'll offer to pick him up and take him out for a drink. He's helping Mona plan Casey's memorial for later on. Isn't that nice of him?"

"So you want me to be at his place sometime Saturday?"

"That's what I said. He rents a town house over on Williams Avenue. You remember that new fancy development they opened last year? I'll meet you there and let you in around six, then bring him back around eight for dinner. Just make sure you're gone when we get there."

"You don't have to worry about that."

"Just put all the expenses on the bill you give me for the Osborne brunch. Here's a deposit so you can get started. I want everything to go right." She took out a checkbook and wrote a deposit check covering far more than was necessary.

"Tanya, this is too much money for a deposit!"

"You know, I've got it," she said with a little smirk, then lit another candle, a not-so-subtle hint that I should be on my way.

A surprise party is always a challenge to pull off. Darryl and I had done our share and something always went wrong. Either a bigmouthed friend spilled the beans, the guest of honor didn't show up or got mad when she opened her door—hair uncombed, in a torn, tacky robe—to confront friends dressed for partying and screaming surprise. Once, an unsuspecting guest of honor passed out cold when he opened the door to face his best friend, whose wife he'd been sleeping with. The surprise almost killed him.

Besides that, I didn't like sneaking into somebody's place uninvited; the law calls that breaking and entering. Did Tyler Chase have a burglar alarm or nosy neighbors? I had no confidence in Tanya's take on their relationship; from what I'd seen she was the enthralled one, riding him like a prizewinning pony at a county fair.

But what did *I* know about men? Tanya Risko had implied, and I hadn't bothered to correct her. There was, after all, the matter of the money. I went back to my desk, called the rental agency, and ordered their best china, linen, stemware, and silver, then planned the menu.

No garlic or onions, Tanya had demanded, so I had to come up with classic *romantic* dishes without those essential aromatics, food that could be prepared at home, plated at his place, and easily reheated in the microwave. I finally came up with seared salmon flavored with thyme and lemon juice served on top of lentil and spinach salad, potatoes roasted with rosemary, and asparagus with hollandaise sauce. (She hadn't mentioned smelly pee, so I assumed asparagus would be okay.) I'd top it off with chocolate mousse trimmed with bittersweet dark chocolate shavings and whipped cream for dessert—with an extra can in the fridge for fun and games.

I texted Tanya the menu and stopped on the way home to buy the nonperishables. I'd pick up the fish and vegetables Saturday morning.

Except for the panting and barking, Juniper is more like a faithful dog than secretive cat. He waits for me to open the door, then follows me around, watches my every move, cheering me up when I'm down. I can always count on him for a chuckle when I need one and a small body to hug when I feel like crying. He lies in the middle of the kitchen floor and is often underfoot. I've stepped on his tail or paw more often than I care to admit, which always brings a squeal and a pitiful look that sends me, guilty as charged, to the cabinet for treats. He doesn't seem to learn—but neither do I.

As always, he was waiting for me when I came into the kitchen, running around my feet nearly tripping me as he begged for his beloved Temptations.

"Get out of the way before I step on you!" I said more harshly than I meant to. He gazed up with a woeful look. Like the devoted servant I am, I put the shopping bag down on the kitchen table and went to the pantry for his treats. "That's all you get for now," I said. He rubbed against my leg to show his gratitude, gobbled them down, then waddled into the living room to fall asleep in his favorite place.

I was surprised when my landline rang; most people call my cell or text. I hesitated before answering it, figuring that whoever it was, I wouldn't want to talk to, and he or she would finally give up. When it rang again, I cautiously answered. It was Louella Jefferson. I knew what she was going to say even before she stopped crying.

Chapter 5

It had been a year since I was in the house where Louella lived with her mother, Bertie, my friend and the coworker who had fooled us all. The place had changed, like everything does. The rooms had been painted for one thing and the smells that lingered that day of old food, anger, and sorrow were gone. Something new had replaced them, and that was Louella's fear. When I'd finally calmed her down last night I promised I'd come to see her this morning so we could talk about what had happened, and now I was here sitting next to her on the timeworn couch, newly upholstered but with a tear in a seam that was bound to get bigger unless it was quickly repaired. It was like Louella's life, which she had only begun to mend.

"Everything was going good, Dessa, until now," she said, as if she could read my thoughts. "I was getting the place together. Red was helping with the painting. We got that new TV, and Erika even helped Red pick it out. She was doing real good in school, too, and now this comes along. It's like life won't give me a break! Red didn't have anything to do with that man's death, but they arrested him anyway. Said he's a suspect, calling me a material witness."

Welcome to the club, I thought but didn't say. I took a quick sip of the tasteless weak coffee she'd brewed with the coffee grinder and French press coffeemaker I'd bought her. It was obvious she hadn't gotten the hang of it yet and ground the beans too coarsely, but now wasn't the time to show her how to do it. I'd bought it for her a few months ago when she closed her first sale, a small deal, but she'd worked hard on it. I figured that was where the money for the paint and couch had come from. I didn't know what Red's contribution had been. I'd wait for her to tell me if she wanted me to know.

"So Red is living here now?" I asked, which seemed innocent enough.

"Off and on. Off when he feels like being by himself and on when he wants to share his life with us. Mostly it's been on, but sometimes he stays at an SRO over on Mulberry Street. He doesn't like Erika to see him there."

An SRO on Mulberry Street? I took a noncommittal sip of coffee; I could certainly understand why he wouldn't want to take his daughter there.

"Erika's in school now?"

"No. She's upstairs. I kept her home today. I've been upset, so I overslept and didn't wake her up. I haven't figured out how to tell her what happened or even if I should."

"You need to tell her something. Never lie to a child, because they always imagine the worst. Tell her what's going on. Her father is back in her life, and she's getting used to him. He can't just disappear again."

"I don't know what to say to her."

"Tell her the truth."

"But I don't know what that is."

"Tell her what you know. She needs to get back to school. Things won't be normal for a while, but at least if she's on some kind of schedule it will be easier for her. You need to get yourself up in the morning and make things okay," I said as sympathetically as I could.

"That's what I want to talk to you about. I need somewhere for Erika to go until this whole thing goes down."

"She needs to be with you," I said, firmly this time. "You need to be together. Erika can spend some time with me, but she can't move in."

"What if they come for me, too? What if they think I had something to do with that man's death? They told me not to leave town, not to talk to anybody. They make it sound like I'm a suspect. What am I supposed to tell my kid? She went through enough last year with my mom, and now this!" Her voice edged on hysteria.

I nodded that I understood but wasn't about to change my mind. I remembered the last time I'd cared for a loved dependent when a caretaker was in legal trouble. Yet Erika was carrying a lot of weight on her eight-year-old shoulders, and I was concerned for the child's well-being. I could see the old glimmer—the deep purple-red shadow that once enveloped Louella—beginning to creep back, not as deep as the one that had been there when I met her, but there nevertheless. Would it never leave her no matter how hard she fought to change her life and forget her past? Would its presence haunt her daughter the way Bertie had haunted her? Maybe it was this house that carried it, with all its suffering stamped into its walls. Like Risko Realty, holding on to grief and rage forever. I touched my mother's talisman, imagining what she would do in such a situation, hoping that her spirit could protect Louella and Erika as it protected me.

"Tell me exactly why they think Red did it." It was time to talk facts, face reality, settle on something solid, and forget the questions my gift was stirring up.

Louella dropped her head, as if it had become too heavy

to hold up. When she spoke, her tone was puzzled rather than accusatory. "Do you remember when Red made that crack about Osborne dying like a rat? It was just something he threw out because he was mad. Somehow the cops found out about it; somebody must have told them, must have let them know that Osborne and Red had history. Do you know who that could be?"

I vaguely remembered Harley saying something about a rat, but thought it best not to mention it to Louella. I'd sure been shocked when Red said Osborne had them, though. Maybe the cops interviewed Harley again. Or maybe it was somebody else. Who else knew that Red and Osborne shared a troubled past?

"Talking about killing a rat is one thing; how did they get from that to him killing Osborne?" I avoided answering her question with one of my own.

She answered, her voice low as if telling a secret, "You know Red works for Rid-Pests, that exterminating company that is always running that dumb commercial about ridding yourself of pests? You know, the one with the rats and roaches dancing around like they're at a disco club and the Rid-Pests guy comes out and waves a wand to make them disappear."

It was so cringeworthy it was hard to forget.

"Well, Red works for them. He's the guy with the wand, and maybe a lot of people would be ashamed of something like that, but it took him a long time to get that job and he was proud of it."

"A job is a job," I said.

"They use poison to kill rats," she continued. "Red uses it in his work. The cops think he got hold of some poison and used it to kill Osborne."

"That doesn't make any sense," I said, trying to reassure her. It was puzzling to me, too. But I didn't know what else the cops had or how Osborne died. I didn't know much about

Red either. Just what Louella had told me, and that Harley had said he had a temper. "How could he have done it?"

"Because he'd been there before. I didn't know it until Red told me later. He'd worked there, and said he had other reasons to go inside the house, too. He didn't tell me why, and I didn't push him. Maybe I should have."

I sipped my coffee, now cold and bitter, waiting for what else she was going to tell me, and finally she did.

"Red spent time incarcerated back in the day before he came home. That was one reason he disappeared for so long. After things fell apart here, he went down south, to Georgia, got into a fight, and had some weed on him. It was just over an ounce, but they threw the book at him. He pleaded guilty and did two years in jail. They're strict down there about stuff like that. Worse than up here. That came up when they ran a background on him, that he'd done some time."

"It's a big jump from an ounce of weed to murdering somebody with rat poison," I said.

"Not if they need to get something on you," she said, which I knew was true. "Not if you're poor and look like Red and you've done time before."

"You said they're considering you a material witness. Did they tell you why?"

"They think I had something to do with it, too, but I didn't. The first time I even saw that man was when he came into the office."

"But you knew who he was when he came," I said, remembering what she told me about Osborne stealing Red's family's property.

"I knew, but I didn't think it was all that serious," she said, but the way she cocked her head hinted that maybe I shouldn't believe her until she added, "I really didn't think Red would get all that mad just because I went there."

"But they didn't arrest you; they arrested him," I said,

hoping to offer some small piece of comfort. "He's the one in trouble, not you."

"For now," she said, her tone low and darker. "I was there with him, they know we're together, so they think I know more than I'm saying, but I don't know anything, Dessa. But because of what happened with my mother, they probably think I'm capable of doing terrible things, too."

"Mommy!" Erika's voice coming from upstairs startled us both, chasing away the painful memory of Louella's past. "Aunt Dessa is here?" She bounded down the stairs and ran toward me with a grin that lit up the room; even the glimmer that had floated around Louella seemed to dim.

Erika had inherited the appealing characteristics of both her parents, but they had taken a distinctive turn on her small, impish face. She had her mother's wide, expressive eyes, but light gray, like her father's, and her toffee-colored skin was dotted with random freckles, giving her a sweet but mischievous look. Her dimples, which broke out whenever she smiled, reminded me of mine and those of my mother, which was endearing. She was dressed as if she were going to a ball in a sequin-covered tulle dress that reached her ankles. A rhinestone tiara was precariously balanced on the top of her head. My guess was she'd dressed herself.

"You look so pretty," I said, hoping to distract her. She was a polite child and acknowledged the compliment, but her mind was somewhere else.

"Is Daddy here yet?" she demanded to know.

"No, he's not."

"Where is he?"

Louella stared at the floor, at Erika, and then at me, lingering longer than she had to as if garnering strength. "We need to talk about that," she finally said.

Erika, knowing something was up, studied Louella, me, then looked back at her mother. Bertie used to brag about her granddaughter being the smartest kid she'd ever known, even smarter than her daughter. She'd gotten it just about right. "Tell me what happened. I want to know now!" Erika demanded.

There was no fooling her. Louella and I both knew she had to tell it straight. This was a hard conversation best had between the two of them. I knew there was nothing I could add to make things easier or painless.

Erika's eyes were shy and frightened as she searched mine for an answer. I had to tell her something before I left.

"You and your mom need to talk, but maybe she'll let you come by on Sunday and I can show you how to make cookies. How's that?"

"What about a chocolate chip cookie cake?" she said, scrutinizing my face for an instant.

"I've never made one before, but we can give it a try." We looked at Louella, waiting for her to give permission, and finally she did, her voice as weary as her eyes.

I didn't have the three cakes and a pie Lennox Royal requested in his e-mail, but I knew that wasn't the point, and I appreciated him for it. What I did have were questions that only he, with his background in law enforcement, might be able to answer. Unfortunately, Georgia, his assistant cook, was at the counter when I walked into his small, popular restaurant. The spicy aroma of simmering barbecue drifted in from the kitchen, making my mouth water. I knew he must be cooking and probably grinning. The comfort of the kitchen was one of the things Royal and I had in common, and the thought of that made me smile. But it quickly faded when I sat down before the unfriendly young woman who eyed me suspiciously from across the counter. When I'd first met Georgia, her possessiveness toward Lennox made me wonder if there was something between them, but the better I got to know him the more I could see that he was not the kind of man to take advantage of the help.

Lennox Royal was a good man, made of the same fine stuff as my Darryl, steadfast and true with a heart that could bleed too easily for his own good—not a wise thing for a former detective to have. He was also strikingly good-looking, and more than one of his female customers routinely gave him an appraising eye of approval. He was tall, well built, with a sprinkling of gray hair on his head and in his beard that gave him a professorial yet approachable look, and his eyes showed more emotion than he probably meant for them to. He listened like a priest to those who wanted to talk and was always ready to feed those who needed something more substantial than words. I knew he was divorced, and there was still sadness in his eyes when he spoke about his wife. I wasn't quite sure what that meant or what had happened between them. He'd also mentioned that Georgia and his wife were friends.

Georgia, neither blind, deaf, nor dumb, knew a good man when she saw one. I wondered if she wished—or imagined—there could be something between them. Whatever her feelings toward him were, she didn't like me, and every now and then an avocado-colored glimmer would surround her, according to Aunt Phoenix the universal sign of jealousy. She had no reason to envy me. Lennox Royal and I were good friends, nothing more than that, and if she knew anything at all about the man, she would know there was only one woman in his life—and that was his thirteen-year-old daughter, Lena, who was autistic.

"Can I help you?" Georgia asked as I settled onto the seat. "You're too early for lunch," she added, sounding suspicious.

"Actually, I'm here to talk to Lennox if he's available." My voice shook slightly, which annoyed me, and I cleared my throat to conceal it.

"Actually, he's busy. Maybe I can help you?"

"I'll just wait for him."

"Could be a while."

"Hey, is that Dessa?" Lennox said as he came out of the kitchen.

"And here he is," said Georgia with a mocking edge as she moved to the far end of the counter.

"I don't think she likes me," I said when she was out of earshot.

"Why?" He was genuinely puzzled.

"If you don't know I'm not going to tell you," I said, slightly annoyed. "Anyway, I came to ask you some questions, and to thank you for your new order. I'll have it together by Monday."

"You know that e-mail wasn't about any order," he said, with a slow smile.

"I know and I appreciate that. I needed to hear it."

"So you're doing okay?" His eyes, wide and as expressive as his daughter's, told me he wanted to hear the truth. I didn't want to insult him with a lie. He didn't have the gift, but he didn't need it.

"No," I said, lowering my voice even further. "I'm not okay. I'm a material witness along with two other people. You remember Harley Wilde from before and Louella Jefferson and—"

"Are you telling me that those people are involved in another murder? Isn't Harley Wilde the boy who was accused of murdering your old boss? And Louella, isn't she the daughter of that woman? Odessa Jones, you've got to get away from that damn place! You've got to cut those people loose!" He used my full name, and that, along with the deep scowl that etched itself on his face, told me he wasn't joking.

I didn't say anything for a while, just studied hard a spot of sauce on the counter that Georgia had missed with her sponge. Truth was, I was unwilling to admit the simple, somewhat painful truth, even to myself. "Those people are family to me now."

"Odessa." Lennox studied me hard before he said my name, which came out sounding like a sigh.

"That's the truth, Lennox," I said. "I see these people, as you call them, every day. I work with them. I care about them. I can't just up and quit. We're tied together for better or worse."

"Sounds like a bad marriage to me," he said with a smirk, "and I've been through one of those. If it's messing with you, destroying a piece of you, or hurting someone you love you've got to cut your losses and split," he added, hinting that he was revealing the truth about his own.

"It's not that bad yet," I said. Or was I afraid of facing an inconvenient truth?

"Okay. You need to do what you need to do," he said, giving in as I'd seen him do with so many folks foolish enough not to accept his advice when he gave it. He went back into the kitchen for a while, and I wondered if maybe our conversation was over, but then he came back with a small pot of tea and two cups.

"Rose hips," he said, "something new I've discovered, since you got me hooked on herbal teas. Lena loves it, too. It's supposed to be good for you, but I just like the way it smells. Here," he said, pouring some into my cup.

"I need something stronger than rose hip tea," I said, and he glanced up at me, his eyes widening with surprise.

"I got some bourbon in the kitchen if you really need it."

"No, this is good," I said, taking a sip. He was right about the fragrance. Rose hips. Its fragrant, flowery taste with its tart aftertaste brought to mind the two major women in my life: my sweet mother, Rosemary. Aunt Phoenix and her acerbic tongue.

"Need some honey? That's how Lena likes it."

"Yeah, I think so." He brought back a jar of honey, which I dribbled into my tea.

We drank our tea in silence before he asked, "What really happened in that kitchen, and why do they think you had something to do with it?"

I took a deep breath, a gulp of tea, and told it all, from my optimistic beginning to the deadly end.

"Let start with the fact that you're a material witness," he said, sounding so much like a judge I felt a sweep of guilt. "A material witness is somebody who has information alleged to be material to a crime, knows something that few, if any, other witnesses do. The fact that you and Harley were in that kitchen when he died would put you both in that category."

"But Louella wasn't there; why is she one?"

"Because she was with the man who they think might have done it. She could have helped him in some way, making her an accessory. A material witness can turn into a suspect with a nod and a wink."

"What about her boyfriend, Red? I think you might know him as Avon Bailey, Jr. He wasn't there either."

"You mentioned Bailey's motive, but he must have had means and opportunity. They checked all those boxes if they picked him up. If he was killing rats then he might have decided he wanted to kill a 'rat' named Osborne. That's one of the first steps in murdering somebody, calling him an animal, making him subhuman. He had access to rodenticide. My guess would be thallium; it's tasteless and odorless. The question is how he got it into him." He was asking himself more than me, becoming the homicide detective he had once been. "That's what they're trying to figure out. The how. That may be how Louella comes into it."

"But she hadn't been in the house before."

"That's what she told you, and folks don't always tell the truth. She may be far more involved than she wants you to know," he said in a way that told me he remembered the events from last year. "Does Avon Bailey have a record?"

"Yeah, but not for something like this."

"What about Louella?"

There was much about Louella's past I didn't know, didn't want to know. She was running away fast from it, and I hoped that glimmer that was chasing her wasn't catching up.

"I don't know," I said because that was the truth.

"Ever heard of generational trauma? Shrinks say that's when devastating, destructive life experiences get passed down in various ways from parent to kid. Sometimes cops make judgments about people loosely based on the idea that the apple doesn't fall far from the tree."

I thought about Erika's frightened eyes searching Louella's face for answers, and the past that haunted both her parents. "If it comes down to that, then we're all doomed by what a parent did," I said.

"Sometimes it's hard to face a reality we don't want to see."

"Yes, Lennox, but there are many ways to know reality," I said, taking umbrage at his tone and sounding more argumentative than I meant to.

"Well, reality is only what you can see, smell, taste, touch, or hear," he said with a touch of condescension.

"Not necessarily!"

"When you find out a new one, let me know," he said, giving a lighthearted chuckle, trying to loosen things up as he headed back into his kitchen.

"Maybe someday I will," I snapped, then hoped he hadn't heard me.

I sat a while longer, sipping the tea that reminded me of Rosemary and Phoenix, trying to figure out how my reality could lead me to who killed Casey Osborne. I knew in the particular way that I dare not share with others that it probably wasn't Red or Louella, but probably was *not* definitely, and I couldn't prove it. If it wasn't either of them, then a murdering somebody was walking around free. And who could that murdering somebody be?

Chapter 6

Lennox's take yesterday on the nature of reality had annoyed me but brought a smile this morning. The man had no idea who he was talking to, and I wasn't about to share that particular aspect of my personality with him or anybody else. Not yet anyway. When you see "glimmers" invisible to others, smell death masked as nutmeg, and have a psychic aunt who sips cherry brandy and quotes Maya Angelou and African proverbs you take *nothing* for granted.

It was Friday morning and the office was empty save for the lingering souls who haunt the place. I said my reverential hellos, then skimmed my schedule. Real estate agents plan their own time, and our days are split between searching for new clients and pleasing old ones. Unless you're rich or are on the verge of a six-figure sale, it's a thankless life based on endless patience, dogged grit, and relentless determination. Most days, I lack all three. I usually do my paperwork in the morning: search for new listings, follow up on leads, mail out preprinted postcards, return enthusiastic calls to those looking for an agent. In the afternoon, I woo possible clients and possible buyers (*possible* being the operative word in both cases). *Occasionally,* the gift will throw me a lead. But only occasionally.

Selling houses, when you can find one to sell, comes down to imagination, skill, and charm—mostly charm. I'm not a good schmoozer. I can't flatter or smile unless I truly feel it in my heart. With me, what you see is what you get, for better or worse. On the other hand, my friend Vinton can grin and beam and work a room like his life depended on it, though it's only his livelihood. Harley always manages to see potential in loser properties and with clever suggestions and passionate zeal turn even the oldest, tackiest, creepiest house into an inviting investment opportunity just waiting for some smart young person to see its potential. Up until she followed me into the Osborne kitchen, Louella was learning valuable skills from both of them.

Each morning when I come into the office, I give myself a pep talk to get started. Fortunately, I had an appointment at two to show a house; unfortunately, the rest of my day was blank. I shuffled through the stacked business cards, absent-mindedly looking for one that would jolt my enthusiasm and turn into a lead. Osborne's fancy embossed cream-colored card dropped smack in the middle of my desk. Anxiety and revulsion swept through me. I quickly tore it up, tossing it into the nearest trash can. Then I realized it might be some jumbled hint from the gift. In the same moment, I thought about Mona Osborne.

I knew from past conversations with my favorite chef-detective that a spouse is usually the first suspect in a murder investigation. So why not the widow Osborne? The cops were convinced that Red, aided by the *wily* Louella, had somehow killed Osborne, but not me. Yes, Mona's snide crack about not confusing her with "some stupid cook" had ticked me off and her uppity attitude rubbed me the wrong way, but why had the cops jumped over her without a second look?

My guess was that there were still men in the world who actually believed that a pregnant lady in a pretty little dress with a pretty little smile (her words, not mine!) was only capable of "taking to her bed" despite her husband lying dead as a roach on her floor. No crying. No wailing, just a moan and a swoon. I'd been so concerned about Aunt Phoenix's peach preserves I hadn't paid much attention either; I was now.

The best way to find out stuff about a second wife is to talk to the first—and that would be my old friend Aurelia Osborne. It was time to follow up on my promise. Luckily, I'd put the card she'd given me with her cell phone number in my bag, and I dug it out now. I rambled on for a minute about what a pleasure it was to have seen her and that I was looking forward to a visit. I said it just happened that I'd be in her neighborhood this afternoon and asked if I could drop by her place for a drink around six, to which she agreed. I decided to surprise her with one of those extra collard green quiches I'd had the foresight to freeze.

The "show house," which was on the outskirts of Aurelia's neighborhood, was a rambling purple Victorian on the verge of tumbling onto a walkway dotted with overgrown weeds. It needed either Harley's vivid imagination or Vinton's winning charm to make it remotely appealing. I quickly roamed the dark rooms, realizing that it was time to question my aunt about houses having glimmers as strong as people. Yet the house did have an odd charm about it, as old Victorians often do. Its gabled roof, turrets, and bay windows might fascinate somebody who loved this style of home. Who knew where an inspired vision and plenty of cash might lead? But I left quickly, hurrying home in time to put the frozen quiche in the oven, taking it out after forty-five minutes. It was appealingly warm when I rang Aurelia's bell and presented it to her.

"Oh, thank you, thank you, thank you," she said, nearly burning my hand with the stub of a cigarette she was holding when she grabbed the plate. She held a drink in the other. Apparently, she hadn't waited for me. The house smelled like cigarettes, with a whiff of what might prove to be black mold. One thing about being a Realtor: You usually can size up a house's market value at first glance. This would be considered a "good" neighborhood. The houses on either side were well maintained and she could probably get a good price if she sold it—at first glance. It was an iron-gray Dutch Colonial similar to the other houses, but the closer you looked the faster the dollar value dropped. The roof needed replacing and a coating of moss covered most of the shingles; the sidewalk and walkway needed major work, too. When I stepped inside I noticed that the living room floor looked uneven. If she was selling anytime soon, she had some work to do, and structural repairs like these were going to cost money.

"You sell houses, don't you?" She must have noticed my expression. She unwrapped the quiche and took a quick sniff. "It's not spinach, is it? Smells like greens."

"Collards. Yeah, I do sell houses. Are you thinking about selling this one anytime soon?" I asked politely, praying she wouldn't ask me to take this one on.

"When things settle down, and I get what's coming to me," she said, with the hint of a grin that she didn't bother to hide. "You know what I mean?"

The silence was uncomfortable, and I needed to fill it. "I'm so sorry about your late ex-husband; I—"

She interrupted me before the words were out of my mouth. "You know better than that."

I followed her into the kitchen, which also needed work, where she dropped off the quiche, and we headed into the backyard.

"We're going to sit out here on the back porch, if that's okay. It's my favorite spot, especially when it's warm, like today. I've got a bar set up, just a card table with all the stuff I like to drink. It's my little bit of paradise back here, you know what I mean?"

I stopped in my tracks on the back stairs, transfixed as I gazed around her yard with awe and admiration.

I love the idea of a garden but never find the time to plant one. Aunt Phoenix is the gardener in my family. Her backyard and windowsills in her small, narrow house are filled with plants and cuttings. Everything she touches seems to bloom, while everything I touch withers. She was an inspiration to both me and Darryl. We dreamed of being the kind of homeowners whose yards overflowed with seasonal flowers—perennials, such as tulips in the spring and annuals like impatiens in the summer. Each year we'd start planning in October in time for planting in April.

Our dream garden would be filled with vegetables, herbs, and flowers, we imagined. Two shelves in our office overflowed with gardening books with advice and tips that we eagerly devoured while sitting in front of our fire each winter. But we never got around to planting more than a few impatiens in May. Each spring and fall, I promised myself I'd honor our dream but never did; it was simply too painful. When I walked into Aurelia's space filled, as it was, with shrubs and flowers, I was lost in my thoughts, and allowed myself the luxury of remembering my past. Aurelia didn't notice.

"If you look around carefully, you see it's mostly shade, except at the end," she said, bringing me into the present. "Those are hostas, different sizes and shapes. They grow good in shady spots. Take up space mostly, and they come back yearly. For lazy gardeners who don't want to plant every season."

"That's me," I said, which was my truth.

She pointed to groupings of deep green and white plants that were spread throughout the space. "The flowers around them, those are impatiens, of course, to brighten things up, and begonias, easy stuff. The flowers over there are flax." She pointed to a group of blue flowers in a partially sunny patch near the house. "I grow them so I can harvest the seeds. My son grinds up flaxseeds and gives them to his father for his and his wife's smoothies. *Used* to give them to him anyway."

"Flaxseeds? They're good for you?"

"According to the late Mr. Osborne. That's what he's told my son anyway. A superfood. You grind them up in a blender and put them in whatever you're drinking. Juice, whatever."

In a sunny spot at the far end of the garden, I noticed a strikingly beautiful shrub, nearly as tall as a tree, with bright shiny leaves that added an exotic, tropical note to its surroundings. I went over to it and touched one of its glossy leaves.

"Remember my aunt Dahina?" Aurelia said, coming behind me. "That one belonged to her, gave it to me when she died. It took me forever to start it and get it to grow good. She raised them back in the Dominican Republic where she came from. I've actually had some luck with this one. Got seeds from it, anyway, which is a very good thing. By the way, how is *your* crazy aunt? Still weird, still casting spells?"

I was taken aback, my back stiffening, and I wondered why she'd said something like that, bringing it up suddenly like she did. Her words were cruel and taunting and made me recall how Osborne had described her when I'd seen him in the office. How much had she changed? Aunt Phoenix was weird, but certainly not crazy, and if she cast spells she kept them to herself. I was sure I had never shared my family's peculiarities with Aurelia; I would have been too embarrassed. But maybe I had. It was a long time ago and we were teenagers eager to share our secrets.

"Okay." I mumbled the word out, too angry to speak. Avoiding her eyes, I sat down on a white wrought-iron bench near the back door. Aurelia must have changed through the years. Being married to a man like Osborne could have done it, or I'd been too young and naïve to see who she really was.

Coming from a place I try *daily* to understand, my phone

rang with a text from Aunt Phoenix, probably with the Pick 4 lottery number or a quote from Maya Angelou. I'd read it later. If Aurelia was right about my aunt, there was no need to let her know it.

"You're not going to answer that?"

"Later. By the way, how is your son doing?" I was eager to change the subject away from my aunt, but I was also concerned. It had been less than a week since his father's death. I understood the grief he must be feeling. He was a kid. I'd been grown. Even after two years, there were days when I felt Darryl's death had happened the day before, like a moment ago when I'd been caught in the memory of our dream garden. Something like that must be going on with this boy.

"Lacey? In his room doing whatever he does. Playing on his PS4 with kids I don't know. Listening to TV with his earphones on. You smoke?" She offhandedly offered me a cigarette. "Oh, I forgot you never did; you were always a goody-good girl, even in high school."

I studied her closely, searching her face wondering again what had happened to bring out this mean-spirited streak. Or maybe it had been there all along.

She joined me on the bench, which was next to the table filled with various liquors, an ice bucket with a bottle of wine, and bar glasses of various shapes and sizes. "You want a martini? That's what I'm drinking." She took a sip from the half-filled glass sitting next to her.

"Wine is good."

"I'll have wine, too, with that beautiful quiche." She set aside her martini and poured us both a glass of chilled sauvignon blanc. I remembered her at the party, with the drink she never put down, and wondered when she had become an alcoholic. What could have been the catalyst? Had he done that to her or had she done it to herself?

When she left for the kitchen to get the quiche, Lacey crept onto the porch, sneaking out so quietly I was startled.

"You were at the party, weren't you?" he asked, his voice cracking. I nodded that I was; out of impulse more than anything I gave him a hug. He looked surprised but didn't pull away like teenagers often do. He was a big boy, taller and more muscular than he looked in the photograph his father had shown me, more like his father than I'd thought. I doubted, though, he had his father's bombast or arrogance. He had a different manner, a softness, shyness, that touched me. I drew back a moment, gaining whatever I could from the gift. There was just the glimmer of absolute sorrow, the one I'd seen on others who had suffered loss, that Aunt Phoenix had seen coming from me but had the tact not to mention.

"You'll be okay," I whispered. "Things will be different, everything will change, but you'll be okay. Try to believe me."

He began to weep like the child he was. I allowed his sobs to come into me, wondering if this was the first time he'd cried like this, letting all his sorrow come out; tears came into my eyes, too. He stopped suddenly, pulled back, his body tightening as his mother came into the backyard.

"Living up to your name, Lacey," his mother said, carrying a tray filled with saucers, the quiche, and silverware. "His daddy wanted me to name him Casey, after him, but I wanted a girl, not a boy, so I kept the name I wanted to give him. Lacey, because I've always loved lace. He's learned to live with it, though, haven't you, Son? Not what his daddy wanted."

I'd wondered about the name when I first heard it, thinking it an odd choice for a man like Casey, and now I knew.

"Yeah, I did," Lacey said, with no expression.

"He's going to learn to live without Casey Osborne, too. Just like he did his name."

I knew that this was not the first time this woman had cut the boy down like this, and I knew it wouldn't be the last. Was that why his father had tried to get custody?

I watched as Lacey's face fell into itself: the slight droop of his head and downward turn of his lips. The glimmer of grief was now one of anger, reddish purple that came, disappeared, yet in that moment it seemed to envelop them both. It made its way into my bones, too, barreling into me like strong emotions do. My first impulse was, as it always is, to leave, get away from them both as quickly as I could, yet I couldn't leave Lacey. He watched me, then turned his gaze away, his eyes following the ivy that traveled up the side of the house. When his gaze came back to mine, I knew we had forged a bond, yet I didn't know where it would lead.

His father's death had left him with nowhere to hide. I'd made an assumption about his family and been wrong. I recalled the scene between the three of them the day Osborne died. How his son had begged to stay with his father, tried desperately to get away from Aurelia. I'd assumed she had dragged her son to the brunch to horn into the party; it must have been the other way around. He'd come there to be with his father and ended up being in the house when he died. The cruelty of that shook me so violently I wasn't sure I could keep it in. Aurelia was the problem parent, not Osborne.

Darryl had told me once about a friend of his, whom he'd loved like a brother but who was too far gone to rescue. The boy's mother wasn't physically abusive, there had been no bruises or cuts, but she showed no emotion and had a cruel heart. Darryl's eyes filled with tears when he explained how over the years he'd watched the woman kill his friend's soul until it was too late to do anything about it. There were tiny cuts and nicks invisible at first, but they grew deeper and more visible the older the kid got until they became calluses too deep to heal. He was hurting other kids by then, including

Darryl, his best friend. It was one of the reasons Darryl had been drawn to helping special children, some of whom he knew he could understand.

"Do you want some quiche? It's good," Aurelia urged her son, trying to wedge a bit between his teeth as if he were a toddler. He shook his head angrily, knocking her hand away. She cut a generous slice for herself and then one for me. I'd lost my appetite.

"Probably too rich for him. He's turned into a real health nut like his daddy was, inspired by his new life and Mona. Always drinking smoothies with all kind of crap in them."

Lacey picked up his head as if just beginning to listen.

"Don't talk about my dad," he said, his voice as wounded as his eyes.

"I'm not talking about your dad; I'm talking about his wife. So why are smoothies good for you, where did he learn that?"

"Dad was trying to get his diet together. He was doing good, Mom. He was eating healthy. He added healthy stuff to his drink, like the flaxseeds and fruit. He was trying hard."

"We should be thankful for that," she said with a slight smile. "When he was married to me all he ate was salt and fat." She shook her head, chuckled, and focused her gaze on her son. "We both should be getting on her good side now. We have to follow the money and see where it goes."

How in the name of heaven could she say something like that to a boy who was hurting so bad? I sipped my wine, avoiding her eyes, which were focused now on me. Lacey left the porch, saying nothing. I watched him leave, his head dropped low.

I was angry but didn't know where to put it because it went so deep. I went into default mode, like I tend to do when I don't want to say what is really on my mind, being polite, taking the comfortable way out.

"So are you going to be okay with everything?" I said, which was the kind thing to say. "I know how things can go after a sudden death like that." But I was sharing more of myself than I meant to; I was wary of her now.

"I really don't know," she said, her shoulders slumping, and for the first time since I'd been there I could see her fear. "Like I said to Lacey. She's his wife, his survivor. She is having a child. I don't know if he left Lacey anything at all. He could be selfish like that. Forgetful."

Not so forgetful, I thought. He remembered his son's allergy to nuts.

She lit a cigarette, inhaled, shook her head as if recalling something sad but worth remembering. "He was something when he was in high school, wasn't he?"

"I guess you could say that," I said.

"I wouldn't have thought we would end up like we did, how bad things got between us."

I nodded as if I understood, took a sip of wine, waited for her to continue.

"He always fooled around, from the time we first got married. You remember him walking down the hall in high school? Girls hanging all over him. Grabbing at him. He ate it all up. I let him have his fun, because he was a star and he knew it and so did everybody else. I didn't let myself care. Later after we were married, he got me anything I wanted, new car, new house, new clothes, took care of us. His fooling around hurt me, but I didn't let it show. He always came home. Until he stopped."

"When did he stop?" I asked, hoping to understand a piece of what had happened, why she had changed.

"They went on for years, him and Mona. She was a hotshot chemist in a small pharmaceutical company he wanted to buy. That's how they met, through her job. She was still working there when he upped and left. Five years ago. She was in her mid-thirties then, probably needed a real commitment from him; you know that baby clock that haunts women in their thirties. Lacey was ten. I was going on forty-two, getting old compared to her."

I thought about Darryl and me then; five years was how long we were married; it went so fast, too fast, and I was changed forever, for the better, or so I hoped. Yet there were days when I was angry and hateful to anyone who crossed my path, blaming everybody else for my unhappiness. I was lucky I didn't have a Lacey to look out for, just myself and a cat. Five years was a long time. Had it changed Aurelia like it had me? If it had, how could I blame her?

"So what's my next move? To be as nice to her as I can be. Let her know we're still around. Send Lacey over there, if he'll go, remind her that the child she's carrying needs a big brother whatever it is, and my son isn't going anywhere. Bring her those little flaxseed mixtures she likes in her smoothies so she'll have a healthy baby."

"Sounds like a good idea," I said.

"Yeah, that's all I can do."

"But I'm sure Mr. Osborne left a will. Mona won't forget his son," I said, but didn't completely believe it. Mona had forgotten the boy's allergy in planning her brunch. Or just didn't care. No telling what she'd forget when it came to money.

Aurelia didn't comment, and we sat sipping wine, enjoying the fragrance of the flowers in her garden, until she turned to something stronger. "You always believed the best about everybody, didn't you?"

"Not always."

"You did about me, right?"

"Yeah, I did."

"What about now?" she said, her eyes looking hard into mine, begging me for an answer.

"We were kids then, Aurelia, and we haven't seen each other in years. I honestly don't know." I said the only true thing I could.

When the Jersey Pick 4 came out on TV later that night, I remembered Aunt Phoenix's text—with annoyance. She was probably right again and I'd missed yet another chance to win some money. But there were no Pick 4 numbers this time, only a quote from Maya Angelou, one she'd sent before:

Bitterness is like a cancer. It eats upon the host.

My aunt and Dr. Angelou were right about bitterness; it was devouring Aurelia Osborne and hungrily waiting to feast upon her son.

Chapter 7

Tyler Chase's town house was part of a poorly constructed development on a dismal back street marketed for "smart" young singles, who couldn't have been *that* smart if they put their money here. The winning point was that it was within walking distance of the railroad station. One of Grovesville's major charms was that it was a commuter town, close enough by train, bus, or car to Manhattan, a perfect fit for those who worked in the city but couldn't afford the rents.

Yet Grovesville had its own particular history and peculiar charm. It was an old Jersey town, incorporated in the 1900s, that had managed to carve out its independence and personality, quite different from the wealthy "sundown town" that adjoined it and the struggling one on the other side. It was lively if you knew where to look but quiet if you wanted peace of mind, which was what had attracted me and Darryl—that and the fact that Aunt Phoenix had settled here long before I was born yet never told me why. One of the many questions about her history my aunt would need to answer someday.

Chase's place was a small corner unit consisting of a galley kitchen, living and dining room area on the first level with a master bedroom, walk-in closet, and full bath on the second.

The property looked reasonably well maintained, but the unit next door hadn't been bought or rented—bad for the owner, good for me. The last thing I needed would be to be caught sneaking out with a shopping bag full of pots and pans.

Tanya's cherry-red Benz pulled up to my ten-year-old Subaru with the subtle purr of a car that cost more than my mortgage, and I was reminded that I was past due a trip to the car wash. Not that it mattered. I was glad the thing was running. But such things did matter to Tanya, who gave me and my car a curt, critical look as she parked in front of us.

But I was bone-tired and didn't give a damn. I'd been up since six, prepping what I could and packing the trunk with the "fancy" glassware, dishes, and silverware my "client" had insisted upon. The Whole Foods in a neighboring town was good for the salmon and fresh vegetables. The store was nearly empty when I got there, so I was able to head home quickly and begin to prep. Starting with the salmon and ending with the mousse, trouble was headed my way.

I seriously overcooked the fish; there's nothing worse than a good piece of salmon cooked to the point where it tastes canned. Tanya would need to be careful when she microwaved it. Halfway through whipping the cream for the mousse I realized I didn't have enough time to refrigerate it properly. I dumped the whole mess in the garbage and made chocolate pudding instead, which would cool in two hours. Tanya had assumed the mousse could be used on her hair, so she wouldn't know the difference. The roasted potatoes didn't let me down—roasted potatoes never do. As for the hollandaise sauce? What madness possessed me to put it on the menu? Butter and lemon sauce would be fine on the asparagus; they'd be too drunk to care one way or the other, and I quickly whipped some up. Tanya had paid for hollandaise, and I was giving her lemon and butter. The chocolate pudding switch was bad enough. Culinary ethics demanded that I tell her about the substitution the moment I saw her. And that was the first thing I said when she stumbled toward my open trunk in what they used to call P-F-M stiletto heels.

"Hollandaise what?" she said impatiently, taking off a shoe and kneading her foot. "Did you remember the whipped cream?"

"Yeah, it's in one of the bags." I'd packed everything into three plastic shopping bags to be hauled into the house. Tanya looked them over indifferently.

"Did you get that fancy silverware—"

"Everything is in the bags."

"Come on then. I'll let you into the house. I have to meet Tyler for drinks, and I don't want to be late. We don't have a lot of time to set things up."

"We?" I said, with unconcealed annoyance.

"You know what I mean." She gave a slight, apologetic smile, but it was clear she wasn't prepared to do much. Decked out in a black satin suit that clung to her body like polyester, she was dressed to seduce. A swath of red lace peeked invitingly from the deep V neckline, revealing a tempting mound of light brown breast. Her heels, as seductive as they looked, were designed to be kicked off at the first available opportunity. After studying the bags piled in my car, she gingerly peeked into the one closest to her.

"Leave that alone; that's the food!" I said, unwilling to let a good day's work drop to the ground if she fell in those shoes. "Take this instead." I pulled out the bag with the napkins and glasses. If she broke a glass, it was on her.

"It looks heavy," she whined.

"Do you want to help or not?" I snapped, too tired to be polite.

"Just wait a minute," she snapped back. She went to her car and returned wearing a pair of black-and-white retro Air Jordans. In the end, the girl had good sense.

It took us nearly an hour to haul everything from my trunk into Chase's town house. Clearly, the man wasn't expecting company. The living room smelled of stale cigarettes and honeysuckle, compliments, I suspected, of Tanya Risko's candles. Ashtrays overflowed with crushed cigarettes, some of which had found their way to the floor. A plush red corduroy sofa covered with matching pillows snaked itself halfway around the cramped living room. Wrinkled newspapers and empty cans of Bud Light littered the glass coffee table sticky with fingerprints, and old magazines were stacked in an untidy pile nearby. A sweat suit had been carelessly tossed on the railing leading to the second floor, hinting of either laziness or a rush to get undressed. The walls were bare of art or photographs, except the wall leading upstairs that displayed a mounted collection of swords and knives fashioned into a macabre floral design that made my skin crawl.

Tanya saw my discomfort. "I told you he collects swords and stuff. He's an expert on fencing. He was like a state champion when he was in high school. Pretty impressive, huh? Don't you love the way he has them arranged?"

"Live by the sword, die by the sword," I muttered without thinking, then realized I should have kept that thought to myself. It must have come from the gift; at least there was no nutmeg. Not yet anyway.

"Why would you say something like that?" Tanya's expression was both hurt and annoyed. "How could you wish something like that on a man like Tyler? You don't know him like I do."

"I'm sorry; it just came out. You've never heard that old saying? I didn't mean anything by it." I feigned innocence.

"No, I haven't heard it, and don't say it again," she said, then added, "Excuse the mess. I keep telling him to get a cleaning lady, but you know how stubborn men can be."

I nodded as if I agreed but kept my mouth shut. I was

still worried that Tanya's surprise dinner—like most surprise events—could be headed for disaster. Yet I reminded myself that past is not always prologue and maybe my bad experiences were just that—bad experiences. I'd never seen Tanya so happy or animated. Had I forgotten how boundless joy fed by new love made you feel? I'd felt that way those first days with Darryl. We were immediately attracted to each other. It was awkward at first, then cautious, and finally fearless filled with the delight that we had found each other. Maybe this was Tanya's chance at happiness after all the losers who had darkened her path. The least I could do was be happy for her. Or pretend to be.

There were parts of Tanya Risko that continued to puzzle me, yet she often surprised me, as if some undiscovered goodness was struggling to fight its way out. Who was I to begrudge her this moment of glee? What did I really know about Tyler Chase—except that he was excessively handsome and a serious slob? I shouldn't hold either thing against him. I watched Tanya humming to herself as she hauled bags of linens, glassware, and dishes into the dining room, pulled a card table out of a closet, and began setting the table. I headed into the galley kitchen to begin my tasks dreading what I would find. I wasn't disappointed.

The sink was piled high with dishes left over from breakfast: two coffee-stained cups, one with traces of red lipstick, a saucer with leftover scrambled eggs and a half-bitten slice of bacon. Tanya hadn't mentioned she'd been here earlier, and I gave her a star for discretion. Cartons from last night's takeout were also still here: leftover sushi, a box of half-eaten rice, two plastic cups of miso soup. A solitary wineglass lay on its side in the dish rack, and what looked like a half-chewed brownie was left on a saucer on the counter. The brownie made me remember the chocolate pudding parading as mousse. I quickly unpacked the container and spooned it into glass bowls, decorating each with whipped cream in the shape of a heart. I placed them next to each other in the nearly empty fridge along with a can of whipped cream and two bottles of champagne.

It's impossible to cook properly in a messy kitchen, particularly one that doesn't belong to you. I had to wash, dry, and straighten up before I could unpack the food and get started. Luckily, the microwave was in working order—after I'd scraped burnt crumbs, embedded sauce, and scum of mysterious origin from the glass plate. I heated the lemon and butter sauce in a small pot tossed in my bag at the last minute, and plated all the food on individual dishes: salmon resting on lentils and spinach, roasted potatoes, asparagus waiting for its sauce. I decorated each plate with garnishes of lemon slices, a sprig of fresh thyme, and parsley, then covered them with plastic wrap with instructions to microwave each individually and to warm the butter sauce for the asparagus. As catering jobs went, this wasn't one of my finer ones, but it was the best I could do under the circumstances.

"Is everything ready?" Tanya said, peeking over the counter that divided the kitchen from the living area. "I don't want to be late picking Tyler up. Did I do everything okay?" she asked with a nervous nod toward the set table. "I should have bought flowers. I meant to bring flowers. Is everything in the right place, Dessa? I mean, he's the kind of gentleman who would notice if I had the forks on the wrong side."

"You have nothing to worry about," I said. Considering the state of this place, flowers and silverware were niceties he wouldn't miss if they slapped him across the behind. Tanya rushed into the kitchen and gave me a warm hug, enveloping me in a flowery jasmine-scented cloud. "Like it?" she asked anxiously when she noticed I'd wrinkled my nose. "It's called Jasmin Noir, Bvlgari. Hundred bucks an ounce. So all I need to do is take everything out of the fridge and put it in the microwave, right? Everything is cooked, right?"

"Pretty much. The salmon is overcooked, so no more than two minutes, just until everything gets warm. The desserts, champagne, and leftovers, if you want anything else, are all in the refrigerator."

She sighed with relief. "Good! I better go. You can let yourself out, okay? But don't wait too long. You can turn off the lights when you go, but leave the one on in the kitchen."

"I'll be out of here as soon as I clean up." It wouldn't take long; the kitchen was in much better shape than I found it.

"Wish me luck," she said in a tiny worried voice that made me smile empathetically.

"Things will be fine. You're really into this guy, aren't you?"

"Yeah. I think he might be the one," she said with a dreaminess that gave me pause.

"Good luck, then," I said, yet I had a twinge of warning that came from that place I can never quite identify.

I tried not to think about that as I finished cleaning the kitchen. I packed up my few pots and utensils, then went down the hall looking for a bathroom. Usually places like this had a half-bath on the first floor. Apparently, this was a cheaper model. I passed by the hideous wall with the sword and knife display, trying hard not to look at it as I headed upstairs. As I suspected, you had to go through the master bedroom to reach the bathroom. I noticed the smell when I entered the room, stopping for a moment to sniff the air. Apparently, Jasmin Noir smelled like roses when it was sprayed into a room.

The bed was unmade and messy, sheets wrinkled, tangled blankets on the floor. Whoever had been here had left in a hurry but clearly enjoyed themselves. I had to give Tanya that—the man must have special talents that had eluded me on first glance. Decorum and respect for their privacy made me drop my head, keeping my eyes to myself, as I made my way to the bathroom.

There was no way to ignore the pale yellow slip and matching panties carelessly dropped on the floor in front of the tub. It was a maternity slip, with an expandable front—and if I was curious about what it was, the inside label "Pea in the Pod" made it clear.

"Oh Lord," I said aloud as I headed back downstairs. It behooved me to get the heck out of here as soon as I could. I just hoped Chase had the good sense and wherewithal to clean up the remnants of last night's escapade before Tanya had to use the bathroom. I hoped she'd be so busy microwaving foods and pouring champagne he'd have all the time he needed.

When I was midway down the stairs, the living room door opened and slammed closed. Were they back already? I stopped where I stood, right beside that horrible sword display.

"You did all this for me?" said a voice I didn't recognize at first, and when I did a gasp caught in my throat. Mona Osborne, using *her* key to enter Chase's town house, was obviously pleased and surprised by the card table set for dinner in the middle of the living room. Too scared to move, I stood where I was, listening attentively as she put down whatever she was carrying and stepped into the kitchen. "You cleaned the kitchen, too? Wow, you're full of surprises tonight, aren't you, baby!"

I considered running back upstairs, hiding out in the oversized walk-in closet. Or concealing myself in the shower. It was early evening, nobody would be taking one now, but even as I considered these thoughts I realized how desperately foolish they were. There was nowhere to go. I was stuck where I was. I had to come out, come clean, before she saw me.

I coughed loudly, letting her know she wasn't alone in the

house before I spoke. "Hello, Mrs. Osborne!" I called out, sounding foolishly cheerful, as I took a step down.

Mona stopped short, staring at me with a wide-eyed look caught between terror and utter surprise. "Are you that caterer I hired? What the hell are you doing here?" She rushed back into the living room and dug through her purse for her cell ready to call the cops. I had to think of something fast.

"Please wait, please, please!" I begged. "You're right. I'm Dessa Jones of D&D Delights, the caterer you hired, and I was hired to cater a surprise dinner for tonight. I was in the bathroom upstairs and I'm on my way out now. I'm so sorry to have frightened you." There was *some* truth in what I said, enough to keep her from calling the cops. She scrutinized me from where she stood, not sure what to think or whether to trust me.

"You did all this, setting the table?" she asked suspiciously.

"I made dinner. It's in the refrigerator!" That much was true, anyway. I heard her step into the kitchen, still clasping the phone, and open the refrigerator. "Now, if you'll excuse me. I just want to get my things and be out of your way." I tried to sound calm and nonthreatening as I came down the rest of the stairs and eased into the kitchen to pick up my shopping bags and dash out as quickly as I could.

I'm not a good liar. These weren't blatant lies but rather ones of omission, so I hoped I could get away with them. I *was* hired to cook a surprise dinner. It *was* in the refrigerator, and with any luck I'd be long gone before she found out the whole story. But a lie is a lie, no matter how it's told, and that moral center that abides inside me, courtesy of my honorable husband, Darryl, and noble mother, Rosemary, told me that I should expect to pay a price for lying—sooner or later.

"Wow, I'm amazed! I didn't think Ty was capable of this," she said with a wide grin and a nod in my direction as if she expected me to agree.

"Well, you never know!" I said, grabbing my shopping bags and heading toward the back door.

But the price of my lies, half-truths though they were, came sooner rather than later.

Tanya's laughter, that little-girl titter she pulled out to charm susceptible men, came first. That was followed by Chase's seductively muttered honeyed little nothings, for all of us to hear. Mona and I saw them enter the house before they did us. For the better part of a minute nothing stirred—not air, nor sound nor breath. Then all hell broke loose. Mona, quick on the draw and a woman of action, made the first move. She violently hurled her cell phone at Chase's head when he stepped into the kitchen. It bounced loudly from his temple to his shoulder to the floor, like a baseball thrown hard and fast.

"Why did you do that?" he asked, eyes wide and unbelieving, as he rubbed his head, then shoulder. "Why would you do something like that?"

What kind of a fool is this man? I said to myself. *Why in heaven's name did he think?*

"I'm not stupid! I'm not that tacky tramp you're doing on the side. You think that's who I am?" Mona's scream turned into a wail and ended with a hiss, like the noise a coiled snake makes before it strikes. I drew back intuitively, sensing an animal ready to attack. Yet Chase simply cocked his head to one side, and grinned as if they'd played this game before and he knew only too well how to handle her—and where it would end up. Those tangled sheets and blankets on the floor upstairs hinted that he was betting right. I didn't want to look at Tanya; I didn't dare.

"So this is what you're going to do, hit me with your phone," he said, taunting Mona, half smile on his ridiculously handsome face. He coolly went to the refrigerator, opened it to pull out a Bud Light, then turned to face her. "Calm down, Mona, before you hurt the baby. Things change," he said, taking a sip. "I told you that from the beginning. Nothing is going to go down like we thought it would. But everything is going to work out. You'll see."

"And you've brought it down to this mess," she said, her voice strangely calm now, an intimate whisper, as if they'd forgotten Tanya and I were standing in the same space. They were in a place that belonged only to them, which told me all I needed to know. Suddenly Chase turned his gaze on Tanya. I made myself look at her now, too. Her face was contorted, her mouth down on its sides as if she was ready to cry but couldn't quite get it out. She began to shudder, slowly, then violently.

"Hey, I'm sorry about this, baby," Tyler said casually. "Sorry it had to go down this way tonight. I hope you believe me. Things will be okay, though. Give me a minute to make things right, and I'll take care of this."

I couldn't tell whether he was talking to Tanya or Mona. As he spoke, he glanced from one to the other, as if he couldn't make up his mind. It was at that moment that I wished, yet again, for the take-no-prisoners, hard-ass gifts of the women Aunt Phoebe called my distant cousins—the ones who with a well-placed blink could take a man down to his knees, with a nod could reduce him to a pool of whatever mess he was made of, with a sweet smile could fry him fast like a pork chop on a hot grill. My meager gifts allowed me only to see the glimmer that surrounded him, and it was one that I never wanted to see again. It was the color of sangria, a bloody purple that grew deeper the longer I stared and made me feel sick. Tanya stared, too, although she couldn't see what I did. She just looked from him to Mona, then back again, finally fixing on the open refrigerator. When she walked toward it,

I was treated again, for the second time in as many weeks, to my well-prepared food becoming a disgusting pile on somebody's kitchen floor.

Winding up her arm like a pitcher at the mound, Tanya began throwing things. She started with the plated dinners, aiming fast and true at Mona, then at Chase, who stood together in muted astonishment as the fancy china dishes bounced, then crashed to the floor in front of them both. Tanya grabbed everything within her reach, tossing things anywhere she could aim. Walls, counters, the floor beneath her feet, were quickly buried in salmon, potatoes, asparagus, and butter sauce. The chocolate pudding came last. Tanya dug her fingers into it like a naughty child playing in mud and pitched a handful hard, first at Mona, who swayed and ducked too late, and then at Chase, who manned up, faced Tanya down, then licked it off his lips.

"This is your damn fault," Mona screamed at Chase, chocolate pudding slipping down her chin. "Look what you've brought down on us. After everything we've been through, everything we planned, and it ends up here with her. Everything I've done for us!"

"Close your mouth! Don't say anything else; I'm warning you." Chase went over to Mona, grabbed her by the shoulders, and shook her hard. "Shut the hell up!" He tried to pull, then finally dragged her out of the kitchen and into the living room.

Tanya, panting loudly, watched them go. Without a word, she pulled one of the bottles of champagne out of the refrigerator and tossed it into the sink, where it crashed, leaving a sparkle of bubbles and glass in its wake. Armed with the other and carrying it over her shoulder like a long gun, she marched out through the back door, slamming it hard behind her.

I stood in the middle of the kitchen floor with the spoils and smells of my food and Tanya's rage surrounding me in a frightening moment of déjà vu. I could hear Mona crying, Tyler yelling, and then the two of them shouting at each other in the living room. Then it was quiet, too quiet. I gathered up my belongings as quickly as I could and followed Tanya out the back door.

I didn't see her at first. I was too busy stuffing my things into my trunk, eager to leave, but then I spotted her, or rather saw her head going up and down in a rhythmic motion against her steering wheel. I knocked on the window, not sure if she heard me. After a moment she rolled it down. Her face was streaked with black tears, her makeup now a bright orange hue.

"Are you okay?"

"Why does this always happen to me? It seems like everything I am, everything I do, turns to crap," she moaned.

"This isn't on you; it's on them. This is not your fault."

"Why did she pretend to be my friend? Why did he use me like he did? Why did they do this to me?" she cried plaintively, searching for an answer.

"You feel like some company?" I asked.

She shrugged and I opened the passenger door and slid in beside her. I took her hand and held it, noticing her long perfectly manicured nails, the same bright red as her lipstick. Just done, I figured, for this special night. She was sobbing hard, and I could think of nothing I could say to comfort her, yet for the first time since I'd known her, I saw her glimmer. It was a soft blushing pink, like the kind a new mother would choose for a newborn daughter or the hope of one. Maybe this was who Tanya was and always had been, not quite grown, not quite formed, someone who had yet to come into her own.

"I wish they were both dead. I wish I could kill them both," she said, becoming a vengeful little girl.

"Don't say that, Tanya!" I said, sounding, perhaps, like the mother she'd never known, and she pulled away like an angry daughter. Sorrow tinged with concern pushed itself into my heart.

"Please go," she said, snatching her hand from mine. "I want to be by myself. Just leave!"

I left her alone without saying anything else.

Chapter 8

I spent the night worrying about Tanya Risko, remembering the sound of her head hitting that steering wheel, wondering if I should have left her sitting alone in the car. She told me to leave, but should I have listened? I could appreciate needing to be by yourself, not wanting folks to see your vulnerability, know how hurt you were. There were days I'd felt that way myself. Sometimes there's comfort in wrapping oneself in aloneness, witnessing your own pain. In the last year, I'd learned to reach out to other people, be open enough to let them see who I was and how I was hurt, and they shared hidden parts of themselves with me, too, and that was how our friendships were born. You had to show your vulnerability so others could show theirs and not be afraid to let you in.

But my truth wasn't Tanya's. She'd opened herself up and look what crawled in. Tyler and Mona had preyed on her susceptibility, and it might be a long time before she left herself that open again. I called Tanya twice before going to bed, asking her to call me back when she felt up to it. If she didn't come to work on Monday, I'd drop by her place to check on her, maybe ask Harley to come with me, although I wouldn't tell him what had happened.

One thing was for sure. After Saturday night's debacle, this morning would be a piece of cake, a chocolate chip cookie cake to be exact. Louella had left a message on my cell reminding me that I'd promised to watch Erika while she visited Red in his room. Erika's high-pitched little voice chimed in the background pleading for us to make a chocolate chip cake. I'd done plenty of chocolate chip cookies in my day but never had a request for a cake. It was no great baking feat, just cookie dough pressed into a cake pan, but only a child would request something like that, and D&D Delights hadn't done much catering for kids. I thought about Lennox's daughter, Lena, who loved cookies and would love something like this. Another treat to add to his dessert menu.

I lay in bed for a while longer, unable to forget Tanya's anguish. Juniper finally brought me into the present, with a well-placed pounce to the middle of my stomach.

"Ow! Stop it, you little pest," I muttered. This was a new trick, a fresh way to get me out of bed when I was taking too long. Up until now, it had been enough for him to cry heartbreakingly and woeful at the edge of my bed until pity got the best of me and I went downstairs to put food in his bowl. But I knew he wasn't hungry. I'd filled his bowl last night, and his water fountain (for which I'd paid a small fortune) was flowing smoothly. He was looking for company, and I was it. Begrudgingly, I got out of bed to meet the day.

I was looking forward to seeing Erika. Her sunny little spirit always cheered me, but I dreaded seeing Louella. There was nothing I could say that would make her feel better. Nothing had changed. Red was still under suspicion. They still couldn't afford a lawyer. He was still wearing the ankle restraint and living in that run-down SRO. They were struggling and probably would be. Erika was the bright spot in both of their lives, as she had been in that of her grandmother.

It was a lot of weight on the small shoulders of a little girl, and I was glad to do what I could to ease her burden.

The doorbell rang twice, with loud thumps on the door in the annoying "shave and a haircut, two bits" knock that only a child would do. I suspected Erika had just learned it. I hurried downstairs to answer the door before she could do it again.

Louella waved from the driver's seat of her car as soon as Erika was inside, then pulled away. She probably didn't want to talk anymore either. There was nothing either of us could say until things were resolved one way or the other. I thought again about last night, and what I'd found in Chase's bedroom. Just because the widow was sleeping with the man's partner didn't necessarily mean she'd killed him. I was sure their relationship wasn't common knowledge, but it should have occurred to someone. Why hadn't the police looked into it more?

Erika was a hugging child and the moment she stepped inside she grabbed me, pulling me down to her level. She was also dramatic; I was reasonably sure she was headed for the stage.

"Thank you, thank you, thank you, Aunt Dessa," she said theatrically with a wave of her hand like the pint-sized drama queen she was sure to become. "Thank you, thank—"

"That's enough, Erika. You're welcome," I said, cutting her off.

She was wearing leopard-skin leggings and a floral T-shirt with the slogan "Don't Pet the Fluffy Cow" scribbled beneath what looked like a long-haired ox. Gone was last week's ballerina/princess. Her black sneakers were laced with bright yellow laces and her hair gathered into a huge Afro-puff.

"What's a fluffy cow?" I asked, genuinely curious.

"They live in Scotland," she patiently explained. Juniper,

sensing the presence of a new warm body, bounded into the living room and rubbed up against her leg. As heavy as the cat was, Erika bent down and managed to pick him up, holding him like a baby. Juniper, never one to scorn attention and play his assigned role, snuggled his nose against her chin.

"I wish I had a cat," Erika said longingly as he leapt out of her arms, heading into the kitchen. "Where's he going?"

"To the pantry looking for a cat treat," I said, with mild disgust.

"Can I give him one?"

"Sure, but just one. He's overweight and eats too many. Do it before we start cooking."

After I showed her the proper way to wash her hands (the method used by chefs and surgeons), we pulled out the utensils we needed—mixing spoon, measuring spoons, a set of measuring cups for solids, a glass measuring cup for liquids. I explained the difference, that solids, like flour and sugar, needed to be leveled off for accuracy and it was easier to measure and pour liquids into a glass container. We lined up ingredients: flour, butter, eggs, sugar, light brown sugar, salt, baking soda, vanilla extract, and, of course, chocolate chips. I put aside powdered sugar, butter, and cocoa for frosting. Erika tore into the bag of chocolate chips, and we both dug in. After we'd "tasted" more than our share, we saved a cup and a half for the cookie cake, Erika choosing a cake pan rather than a pie pan. "We are baking a cake, not a pie," she reminded me after generously spraying the pan with cooking spray. I lined it with parchment paper—a safeguard against sticking. I hauled out my *serious* mixer—a KitchenAid Artisan. Erika was impressed with all the attachments, particularly the paddle attachment that we chose to use. I set the oven at 350 degrees, popped a stick of butter into the microwave to soften for the batter—five seconds on each side—and we were ready to roll.

A chocolate chip cookie cake is basically a giant chocolate

chip cookie with a bit of baking soda added to give it some rise. After the butter, sugars, eggs, and vanilla were beat until fluffy, we added the dry ingredients and beat on low until mixed. Erika stirred in most of the chips by hand, saving some to place on the top. She sprayed her hands with cooking spray and pressed the stiff dough into the cake pan in an even layer, using the leftover chips to form a smiley face (her choice, not mine), and it went into the oven. She pulled over a chair so she could watch it bake through the oven window.

"How long will it take?" she asked after two minutes.

"Until it's golden brown."

She sighed impatiently and was soon joined by Juniper, who settled down at her feet to keep her company.

The cake had about twenty-five minutes to go when the doorbell rang. I assumed it was Louella, come to pick her up early, but I was wrong.

Lacey Osborne, brown corduroy backpack swung over his shoulder, stood anxiously waiting for me.

"Here," he said, handing me the backpack when I opened the door. "You left it at my house and I wanted to bring it back because I thought you might need it."

"The backpack?"

"No, what's in it," he said with a smile that slowly widened. "It's the dish you brought the quiche in, when you came over."

"Right," I said, remembering it. I'd been so disturbed by Aurelia's treatment of her son and in such a rush to leave I'd completely forgotten it. When I opened the backpack, I found she hadn't bothered to wash the dish. I didn't hide my surprise.

"Sorry. I was supposed to do it, but I didn't," he said, noticing my expression. "I have a lot on my mind and I just didn't get around to it."

"No big thing," I said, as he stood shifting from foot to

foot uncomfortably as if he didn't know what to say. I filled in the silence. "Thanks for bringing this back."

He shrugged. "No big thing," he said, in the same tone, and we smiled as if sharing a joke.

"You rode your bike over?"

"Yeah. My mom was going to see Mona and finally said I didn't have to go if I didn't want to. She went over there to take her some stuff and talk."

"And you didn't feel like going?"

He nodded. "I remembered your dish, so I put it in my backpack and decided I'd drop it off."

"Thank you for thinking of me," I said, knowing that more than anything else, the boy probably just needed someone to listen to him, and I was grateful to be that person. We both knew it wasn't about my old pie pan.

"We had a big fight, me and my mom, about me not going with her. I don't know what to think about Mona and I didn't want to see her."

I nodded, as if I understood, and waited for him to continue. "My mom is probably still over there. Making tea, bringing her food, like she'll even eat it, being nice 'cause my mom's scared she won't give us any of my dad's money. I don't care if she does. I don't want anything that belongs to her. Or that stupid baby," he said, his voice as hateful as the look in his eyes suddenly turned.

"Try to see the bright side, Lacey. Soon you will have a little brother or sister; isn't that a good thing?" I asked, even though I knew that might not really be the case, at least when it came to blood, and wondered if he had guessed as much. I couldn't forget Chase's warning for Mona to be careful about the baby, as if he was invested in its welfare. Lacey was a smart, observant kid not easily fooled.

His refusal to answer told me everything I needed to

know. "You baking cookies?" he asked, looking me straight in the eye, determined not to comment one way or the other on the baby.

"Yeah. Cookie cake, actually. Chocolate chip. It's in the oven. You want to hang around and wait for a piece or I can cut you some to take home."

"Does it have any nuts in it? I'm deadly allergic to nuts."

"No, just chocolate."

"Sure," he said. "I'll wait. Can I leave my bike where it's at?"

He had left it lying haphazardly on the edge of the sidewalk directly in front of my house. I could tell by looking at it that it had cost somebody close to a grand and just waiting for someone to trip over or steal it.

"Do you have a lock for it? Put it in the backyard and lock it up. If not, I'll put it in the garage."

"I have a lock. My dad made sure he got a good one when he gave it to me for my birthday."

"Good. I'll wait for you here."

He moved his bike off the sidewalk into the yard, locked it up, and rushed into the house, heading into the kitchen. It was then that it occurred to me that the daughter of the man accused of murdering his father was sitting in front of the stove, and that maybe inviting this boy into the kitchen wasn't the wisest thing to do. Lacey stopped dead at the door, reared back, his eyes wide with fear. Had he seen Erika? Could he be afraid of her, not want to face her? She was half his size and weight, but maybe it was everything that had recently occurred, and the sight of this little girl brought it all back. It had only been a week. Just a week, and that was no time at all. Surprised and alarmed, Erika stared at Lacey from where she was sitting.

"I know who you are," she said, her voice unnaturally solemn. Juniper, who had followed her into the kitchen, edged closer as if to comfort her. Or did his cat instinct tell him something else, was he protecting her? "I'm sorry about what happened to your dad. But my daddy didn't hurt him. He didn't kill him. I promise he didn't do that."

Lacey slowly, step by step, backed out of the room. Juniper lurched away from Erika toward Lacey, who quickly moved farther back. "I'm scared of cats," he said, his voice small and frightened.

"I thought maybe you were scared of me because of my dad?" Erika said, studying him closely, her eyes big with concern.

Lacey turned toward her, suddenly indignant. "No! You're a little kid; why would I be scared of you? It's the cat. I'm scared of that stupid cat!"

"Juniper?" Erika asked in disbelief, leaping to Juniper's defense. "Don't call him stupid! He's smart and nice. He won't hurt you."

"A cat scratched up my face when I was a baby, a real little kid, and I've been scared of them ever since. I don't like cats. I don't trust them, and they don't like me."

"But he's nice!" Erika said, pleading Juniper's case.

"Juniper!" I warned, coming into the kitchen as he crouched toward Lacey. Like all predators worth their salt, he had sensed the boy's fear and had decided to show off his street creds. He glanced at me, then Erika, and finally at Lacey and bounded past us out of the room. "I'll put him upstairs," I said, going after him.

"See you later, Juniper." Erika reluctantly waved.

"Good riddance," said Lacey, moving cautiously into the kitchen. "Do you have any more?"

"He's it," I said, running to catch Juniper, who had turned as slippery as a greased pig. Defiantly dashing through the living room and up the stairs, he avoided me at every turn until

I finally grabbed him, deposited him in my office, and headed back downstairs.

"I know your dad didn't kill my father because I know who might have," I heard Lacey say to Erika as I approached the kitchen. I stopped at the door, eager to hear more.

They sat close to each other on kitchen stools in front of the oven, watching the oven window as the smell of freshly baking chocolate chip cookies filled the room. I stood outside, curious to hear what else they were going to say.

"If you know all that, then how come you don't tell the police so they can let my daddy go?" Erika asked.

"I want to be sure. I need to get proof."

"What does proof mean?"

Lacey chuckled condescendingly. "You really are a kid, aren't you!"

"A smart kid," said Erika, cocky and cool.

"Proof means finding something that proves somebody did it. Like poison or something. That's how I think she did it, with poison."

"Who?"

"Who do you think? My stepmother."

"Is she like the cruel stepmothers in stories?"

Lacey shrugged. "She's kind of all right some of the time, I guess."

"How could she find poison?"

"She'd know where to get it. She used to be a chemist before she married my dad. You know what chemists do? They make medicines. She probably mixed something up and gave it to him when he didn't know it."

Erika was quiet for a moment, then asked, "How are you going to find out?"

"I know who to ask for help. My dad's partner. We're friends, and he's cool, and he loved my dad, too."

"What are you going to do when you get the proof?"

"I'll make her pay for what she did. My dad always told me never to be afraid of the truth, don't run from it, don't be scared."

"Sometimes it's okay to be scared. You're scared of Juniper," Erika teased, reminding him of what happened earlier.

"But I'm not scared of this," he said.

"I get scared sometimes. I'm scared my daddy is going to go to jail. What do you do when you're scared?"

"I ride my bike," Lacey said after thinking for a moment. "I just ride fast trying to be invisible. It makes me feel close to my dad because he gave me that bike for my birthday last year."

"Where do you ride to?"

"Mostly the park because me and him used to ride there all the time. It makes me feel good seeing stuff that we saw together. I ride until I can't ride anymore, don't have to think about things anymore."

Neither of them said anything for a while, just sat in the warm kitchen watching the cake brown. When Lacey spoke again, his voice trembled. "My dad died last week, seven days ago. I can't believe he is gone."

"My dad left, too, before I was born, but he came back." Erika spoke gently, in her own small way trying to offer comfort, that maybe what had happened to her would happen to him as well; there was no comfort to be had.

"My dad isn't coming back because he's dead."

What did Lacey know about his father's death? Was it something that might put him in danger? Should I mention it to his mother? What would I say? She'd probably accuse me of sticking my nose in her business, dismissing his words as those of a grieving kid running his mouth. Maybe that was all he was.

The oven timer broke the silence, ending the somber mood that had settled in the room. I coughed to announce my presence, then came in to take the cake from the oven so it would cool. Both youngsters were lost in their thoughts, excitement about the cookie cake gone.

"Do you want me to decorate it?" I asked to no enthusiasm. Taking it upon myself, I whipped up a quick chocolate butter frosting, spooned it into a piping bag fitted with a star tip, and when the cake was cool piped small decorative mounds of frosting around its edges. I cut and wrapped a generous piece for Lacey. He thanked me, gracing me with an unexpected hug, then tucked it into his backpack and got on his bike to head home. I watched him ride away, wondering again if I should call his mother. But exactly what had I overheard? Two kids talking, a teenager grieving the loss of his father, a pledge steeped in grief about finding proof.

Erika was in a pensive mood, a rare thing for her. I wrapped up most of the cookie cake, and we sat together at the table with two glasses of milk eating the rest. When we finished it, she eyed the mixing bowl with the remaining frosting.

"Do you think Lacey will find proof of who killed his dad so they can let my daddy go?" she asked.

I nodded and handed her the bowl and a spoon. "It may not be Lacey, but I'm sure that somebody will find the truth."

She sighed as if she understood, focusing her attention on the chocolate frosting stuck at the bottom of the bowl and thoughtfully scooping it up with her spoon until it was gone.

"What if nobody finds it?"

"We'll just have to wait and see," I said, trying to sound hopeful, but I knew it was a poor answer for a little girl who desperately needed more.

Chapter 9

After Aurelia on Friday, Tanya on Saturday, and Lacey on Sunday, the week that followed was blessedly calm. I showed some houses, made some calls, sent some postcards. Harley, delivering my double latte, and Vinton, toting a bottle of merlot, both dropped into the office on a couple of days to chat, use the fax, and pick up letterhead. Their gifts were tokens of affection, and I appreciated them. Neither one mentioned the catastrophic brunch of two weeks ago. I appreciated that, too. At one point, I asked Harley if he'd heard anything from the cops; he shrugged and seemed reluctant to answer, so I didn't push it. If he had something to tell me, he would. I hadn't heard anything either, much to my relief.

We were all worried about Louella, who came in once or twice during the week after dropping Erika off at school. She didn't say if her daughter had mentioned anything about Lacey's surprise visit, so I assumed that Erika, wise child that she could often be, had kept the visit to herself. Louella did say she was late paying her bills and her Wi-Fi was going to be cut off, and we all chipped in to help her out with that. I was happy she was getting Erika up and out in time for school each day, but her lingering fear about Red's fate still hung around her in a grayish shroud. Tanya was working from home, as she put it, and kept in touch with us through group e-mails, one announcing that she was planning to "grow" our workforce and was on the lookout for new agents. "IF RISKO REALTY IS GOING TO SURVIVE, OUR FAMILY NEEDS NEW BLOOD," she wrote—all in caps. Maybe she was right, although I'd gotten used to the comfort of being a member of our small group. Knowing Tanya's history of misjudging character, I was wary of welcoming too many new "family" members without one of us vetting them.

But the week was done, and things were quiet as they often are on a Friday morning. After greeting the "beings" who inhabit this place, I leaned back in my chair enjoying the last of the coffee I'd picked up on the way over and savoring the quiet peace of the empty office. I was scheduled to visit the ladies from the Aging Readers Club late this afternoon to plan a menu for their annual luncheon and was looking forward to that, although I did have a certain degree of anxiety, considering the disasters of my last two catering jobs. But as Laura had told me last year when I first met her, one had to keep hope alive, and that was what I was banking on.

I'd just finished jotting down some preliminary luncheon menu ideas when I felt a slight, quick chill, which can on occasion forewarn that something or someone unexpected is heading my way. Not all sudden chills were bad; some were simple alerts cautioning me to be prepared. This was one of those. Aunt Phoenix, dolled up in her going-to-town apparel, walked through the door.

My aunt, with a wishful eye toward summer, wore a natty seersucker pantsuit that looked as if it had been bought a while ago but still fit her well. Her bright pink blouse provided a bright contrast and a matching pink turban covered her short dazzling white hair. She finished the look off with silver hoop earrings that made her look two decades younger. My aunt's fashion choices had no rhyme or reason. I'd seen her in everything from long flowered muumuus often paired with a blond pageboy wig to a chic black suit touched off with flame-red long hair. She nodded, sat down in the chair next to me, and gave the office a slow once-over. I wondered why she was here and what she was looking for. In terms of that forewarning chill, I wasn't out of the woods yet.

I love my aunt dearly but often have a fleeting sense of anxiety during our encounters because I never know what she will say. She's a teller of truth, when I'd rather not hear it, and never sugarcoats her words when a spoon of honey would make them go down easier. I'm never sure what to expect from her, which can be a troubling thing.

"You look nice!" I desperately needed to fill what had become a lengthy silence.

"No need for that, Odessa," she said with the slowest of smiles, turning to look me in the eye. She leaned back, taking her good time before she spoke. "Whatever happened is gone, and those left can do no harm. But it's wise to give them their due each morning as you do. That's all they expect."

As always, she knew things I didn't need to tell her.

"There's still a lot of trouble in this place and more is probably on its way." She glanced toward Tanya's office. Whatever it was, I didn't want to hear about it, not today anyway.

"Aunt Phoenix, I'm really glad you dropped by, but I do have a lot of things on my calendar—"

She gave me a look that said she knew I was lying. "Where's Rosemary's gift? The one you wear?" she asked bluntly, distinguishing the talisman from the other ones.

As luck would have it, I'd forgotten it this morning. "Do you think I need it?"

"You always need it. Now tell me what's going on and why I haven't heard from you."

"But you never hear from me; I hear from you," I said. She was always the one who called or texted.

She chuckled again because she knew I was right. "I may have a client for you. The Weatherbees. They're looking for a new house and I gave them your name."

"Where do you know them from?" I asked, suspicious. "They're not *family,* are they?"

"If they are, they're very distant. They're friends of Selma Wells, the lady next door."

"I thought you two had a falling-out."

"We did, but we're fine now. We always make up. We're neighbors, best not to fight with your neighbors. In fact, Selma gave me a shrub last week that she had to get rid of to replant in my garden. It's a beautiful one, but a bit large for my space. It's supposed to earn its own keep."

"Earn its own keep? What does that mean?"

"I'll see, but it's an interesting plant, and I'll give it time. She mentioned that they're looking for a special kind of house. Something unique and older with personality."

"I know just the house," I said, recalling the one I'd seen on the way to Aurelia Osborne's last Friday. "Thank you, Aunt Phoenix, but you came all the way over here to tell me that?" I looked her dead in the eye, demanding the truth; two could play this game.

"No, I want you to come to brunch on Sunday. It's my birthday, and I thought I'd celebrate this year."

"Special birthday?" I had no idea how old my aunt was but decided the question was worth a risk. Her answer was a slightly raised eyebrow. "Do you want me to make you a cake?" I quickly added.

"No, just bring champagne so we can have a toast. Birthdays deserve a toast. Even in the afternoon. Make sure it's good champagne."

"Champagne? You've always struck me as a Bloody Mary kind of girl."

"I shouldn't strike *you* as any kind of a girl," she said, putting me in my place. "I got used to drinking champagne when Celestine was here last year. Maybe we'll do a FaceTime toast." She paused for a moment, as if something weighed on her mind, then added, "You had quite a weekend, didn't you? Don't ask me how I know because I do. I just want you to heed this advice, Odessa: Take it easy. Let things lie as they fall. Mind your own business. Don't look for trouble. Stay out of harm's way."

My back stiffened, remembering that chill.

"I don't know for sure, but sometimes my gift fails me, too," she continued, noting my reaction. "Sometimes age makes it stronger, but sometimes it can dim it, like my hearing. You need to be careful, Odessa. People are not always what they seem." She nodded at the place where Bertie, Louella's mother, once sat.

"Does this have something to do with Louella and Red?"

"Who?" she asked, her face going blank. "Don't forget about Sunday. I have some rosemary cuttings for you that remind me of your mother, and my bearded irises are in bloom. I know you love them, from the first time you saw them, remember when you were a little girl? You used to say they were the most beautiful flowers you'd ever seen."

That memory brought back my mother, too, and those strange days we'd lived in my aunt's little house. Her gaze dropped from mine, probably back to that younger sister, whom we both had loved so much.

"I assume you want me to make brunch?" I changed the subject to lighten the mood.

"Of course, but something simple," she said as she left, bestowing a quick kiss smelling of Chanel N° 5 and cherry brandy.

* * *

I remembered my aunt's words later that day when I rang Laura Grace's bell, although I doubted that she or the other ladies in the Aging Readers Club, or the ARC as they called themselves, had anything to do with her warning. Laura Grace, the founder, lived next door to Harley, and when he'd been in trouble last year she and another member had rescued him from the eager clutches of the law and considered themselves his guardian angels. The members were mostly retired librarians and teachers who met each month to discuss books and current events and drink tea or whatever was offered. *What do we do? We drink, we read, and we know things,* one member joked when I met them last year. The tea was usually Earl Grey or Constant Comment and the drinks changed according to the season—mimosas in the spring, eggnog in the winter, gin and tonic in the summer, and red or white wine depending upon the weather and their mood.

"Perfect timing, my dear, we're all here, just finished our meeting, and you're just in time to talk about our luncheon menu!" said Laura Grace as she ushered me into her living room, an oasis of subtle good taste. The cream-colored walls trimmed in white were a perfect backdrop to the two plush brown velvet sectional couches where the members sat, and the white bentwood rocker that Laura settled back into. It reminded me of my aunt's bentwood rocker except somebody had paid a pretty penny for this one as opposed to finding it in a secondhand shop, so the resemblance stopped there.

"We call it our drunken luncheon, because we serve lots of wine and drinks for those who want them," said Clara Berg, whose short bobbed hair was the same shade gray as Laura's and whose dark eyes darted back and forth like a bird's.

"I hope we're not getting an unruly reputation, but the booze does flow, people do let their hair down—what's left of it anyway—and everyone does have a good time." said Margaret

Sullivan, the tall, thin blonde who was with Laura at Osborne's party and who had played a part in Harley's rescue last year.

"So what are you offering and how much money are you talking about?" said Laura, getting right to the point. I presented my menus according to price range, beginning with the least expensive: finger sandwiches, varied quiches, salad greens, fruit salad, and sugar cookies for dessert, ending with the costlier fare: chicken piccata, wild rice pilaf, roasted carrots, asparagus, green salad, and mini cheesecakes.

"Cheap is okay; then we can spend money on good spirits. There is nothing worse in this world than cheap wine, and you can tell in the first sip," said Clara. The other ladies nodded in agreement.

"We do have our standards," sniffed Margaret Sullivan.

"Okay, let's go with finger sandwiches, the quiches, green salad and some kind of fancy fruit salad, and cookies," said Laura, getting back to the point.

"I can do something called a piña colada fruit salad, which is tasty and different."

"I loved that quiche you made at the Osborne luncheon. Can you do that again?" asked Margaret Sullivan.

"Or maybe not. We don't need that kind of bad luck," snapped Laura, then noticing perhaps how my face dropped in obvious discomfort, asked gently, as if prying an uncomfortable answer from a reluctant third grader, "Did everything resolve itself or are things still up in the air?"

"Up in the air," I said, evidently sounding like a distressed child, because the club members, all women who cared about kids, leaned protectively toward me, as I imagined they once had done for some needy youngster who had wandered into their midst.

"But the killer has been arrested, right?" asked Clara Berg, her dark eyes looking piercingly into mine.

"They arrested someone, but . . . who knows for sure."

"What do you mean by that?" Margaret asked with a scowl.

The question hung in the air without an answer. I clumsily changed the subject. "I was so glad to see you-all there. I shouldn't have been surprised, though. Mr. Osborne told me how many important, smart people he had invited." It was awkward and obsequious, unworthy of the company. Laura, taking pity on me, picked up the ball.

"Actually, he didn't invite us. He probably wouldn't have considered us rich enough for his list. She did, Mona Osborne, and she only invited me. I didn't want to go alone, so I bullied Maggie into coming with me."

"You owe me one for that," Margaret reminded her.

"And I know you won't forget it," Laura replied.

"Mona Osborne?" I asked, bringing the exchange back to where it started.

"Mona Osborne. I remember her, poor thing," said Clara Berg, moving in closer ready to share a secret. "God, how many years ago was that? She was in my kindergarten class. I don't think I've ever seen a child go from happy to sad so quickly."

Laura came back from the kitchen with the wine, emptied what was left into our glasses, and settled back down in her rocking chair ready to say more.

"Mona's mother and I were friends, not close friends but acquaintances, and we belonged to the same social club. We lived near each other, and I've watched Mona grow up. Every now and then, she'll reach out to me in memory of her mother, I suppose. But I was surprised to get her call inviting me to her brunch. Maybe she needed to see a familiar face, although I haven't played that part in years."

"Her mother died?" I asked.

"Of a broken heart. Some hearts break slowly, piece by piece, and Annette's broke like that. She never recovered after her older daughter, Millie, took her own life, and I'm not sure if anybody in that family ever mended. Slowly, but very surely, it took its toll. You never recover from the suicide of a loved one, especially that of a child. Mona had a front-row seat to her mother's deterioration."

"Her name was Millie?" I asked.

"Millicent. We called her Millie. Annette's oldest daughter, Mona's teenage sister. She killed herself over some boy or something like that; that's what Annette believed, anyway. Some football player who went to her school."

My breath caught in my throat. "I remember that. I was in high school then, and I remember when she died. The whole school was torn apart."

"Not quite. They had one or two grief classes; then the whole tragedy was forgotten. Then you must know who that boy was."

I nodded that I did. Laura hesitated, as if remembering something unpleasant, then took a few sips of wine before speaking again. "And the crazy thing about all this is that not until I got home after drinking all those mimosas did I realize that Mona's husband, the host of the party, must be that kid her sister was so in love with. Why would she do something like that, marry the man who her mother thought was responsible for her sister's death? I don't understand," she added with a sigh and a puzzled shake of her head.

"She was a little kid when it happened," said Clara, offering an explanation. "Or maybe he felt guilty about her sister's death and made a point of reaching out to her. Or maybe she reached out to him for some kind of closure or who knows?" She shook her head in exasperation. "Life has too many crooks and turns and alleys for anyone besides God to keep track of why people do stuff like they do."

Or maybe she just wanted to get even, I thought, but kept that notion to myself.

"And let me give you another twisty turn," said Margaret, leaning toward the group with more information. "Osborne's son, Lacey, was in one of the very last classes I taught before I retired. He was smart but a bit . . . troubled."

"Troubled?" I asked.

"Are you talking about the fires at the school?" asked Clara.

"They never definitely tied him to those, but I think we all know the truth," Margaret said.

The women glanced at each other and then at her and finally at Laura, the leader of the group, who shook her head, almost imperceptibly, as if warning Margaret not to go any further.

"They never definitely tied him to those and none of us really knows for sure," Laura said.

Margaret continued anyway. "I will say this, though, and I do know it for sure. Lacey Osborne's interest in fires and swords and knives was completely inappropriate for a child his age. I'm going to leave it at that."

The ladies nodded in unison, each taking a sip of whatever she was drinking, and they all left it at that.

Chapter 10

Tanya Risko was the last person I expected to see this early on a Saturday morning. I was stretching long and lazily, eager for that last bid for sleep before starting my day. Even Juniper hadn't yet made his morning dive into the middle of my stomach. When the doorbell rang five times, no less, I feared it was an emergency but couldn't for the life of me figure what it was about. Had something happened to Aunt Phoenix? I rushed into the bathroom, ran a washcloth over my face, noticing with irritation that the silver streak of hair I occasionally get on the side of my face for no apparent reason had come in overnight. Pulling on a robe, I dashed downstairs to open the door. Tanya stood shaking and crying on my front porch.

"I can't believe it! I keep seeing his face in my head. Remembering what we had together, how good things were between us!"

I drew in a long breath, let it out slow, said a quick prayer for patience. "Tanya, what happened to you and Tyler was a week ago. You're imagining things. It was a terrible experience, and you've got to get over it. He is not worth your trouble. Put it behind you! Tyler Chase and Mona Osborne are out of your life. It's done," I said, as firmly as I could. "And it wasn't good between you or it wouldn't have gone down like it did," I couldn't help adding.

She stared at me, eyes incredulous. "You mean you haven't heard?"

"Heard what? Tanya, what are you talking about?"

I ushered her into the living room and sat her down on my couch. She closed her eyes, then opened them again as if waking up. I was snatched back to an afternoon a year ago when I'd been confronted with an equally distraught Tanya Risko hysterical over the horrible, if well-deserved, fate of a former lover. Something told me (call it the gift if you must) that I was witnessing another round of Tanya's misfortune with men. I knew I had it right when she grabbed and squeezed my hand so tightly I thought I might need to pry off her fingers.

"Tyler is dead! He's gone, Dessa! It was on the news last night; they found him in his place, and it was on fire! Do you think I caused it? Do you think maybe I made it happen? I really loved him, Dessa. I really did, but I wished him dead, and I meant it. I wanted him to die!"

"What? Are you serious? What did they say?"

"His place was on fire and he died there!"

I sat down, letting it sink in for a minute. "Listen to me." I grabbed her shoulders and forced her to look at me. "If wishing a man dead was all it took to kill him, half the men in Jersey would be in graves. You need to lie here on this couch while I go into the kitchen and make myself a cup of coffee and you a cup of tea. Then you need to tell me everything you know about what happened to him, do you understand?"

She nodded meekly, took off her shoes like an obedient child, and stretched out full length on the couch. Juniper jumped beside her and burrowed down next to her. I tried to nudge him away, but he was determined to stay.

"No, leave him," Tanya said. "He makes me feel loved."

Truth was, she was in one of his special spots, but I saw no need to tell her. "Wanna take him home?" I said instead, and a faint smile appeared. The smile disappeared as she leaned toward me, focusing on my face.

"God! How come you did that to your hair?" she said. "Is that some kind of weird, desperate fashion statement?" she asked, seemingly forgetting about the reason she'd rushed over to see me.

"No, it comes out of nowhere," I said, giving her the truth because I couldn't come up with a plausible lie.

She screwed up her face, continuing to stare. "What do you mean? That's really strange. How the heck could it come out of nowhere?"

"It just does, Tanya," I said, not hiding my annoyance.

"Why don't you just dye it?" She stared a bit longer, then lost interest. "Maybe I should get myself a pet, a dog, a cat, or even a bird like that stupid one Harley has. Someone that I can love and I know will love me back," she said, suddenly turning thoughtful and petting Juniper.

"I wouldn't get a bird," I said, remembering Parker, Harley's parakeet. He'd been a noisy mixed blessing when he'd stayed with me during Harley's absence last year.

"Is that why people have kids, to make sure they'll always have somebody around to love them?" she asked, dead serious.

"No. People have kids because they're a blessing and they're cherished because of that, not to keep them company," I said, annoyed with her again and sounding more angry than I meant to. Unknowingly, she had scratched a raw piece of my heart about not having children, one of the many losses I'd felt since Darryl's death. Instinctively, I drew away from her as I often do to protect myself from someone who means me harm, although I knew she was no threat; she didn't seem to notice.

"I wasn't anybody's blessing, and nobody cherished me," she continued, sulking again.

"Then you've got to learn to cherish yourself," I said curtly, and went into the kitchen to keep myself from saying anything else. Juniper followed me, having given up on getting his spot back. I made myself some coffee and a pot of tea for Tanya—chamomile and lemon balm, with some valerian for good measure. Valerian being Aunt Phoenix's go-to herb to put you to sleep or quiet your nerves.

"It's nice here," Tanya said, sitting up and surveying the room when I came back. "It's got a good vibe. *Vibe.* That's the word my Pa Nettie used to use. *Vibe,* like 'so-and-so has a nice vibe.' It means like something is good, calm."

"Thanks," I said, as I poured her a cup of tea. *Vibe* was one of those words that Darryl used every now and then and she was right; our place did have good vibes. My mind went back then to that place where Darryl lives. We'd bought everything here secondhand or on sale, comfort and price always mattering more than style. We were amazed when everything fit together, like we actually had a design. The two soft-gray easy chairs in front of the fireplace were a nearly perfect match to the small couch, a darker shade of gray, placed farther away. The fireplace, with its black andirons abandoned by the previous owner and its white brick mantle, always drew attention. After some discussions, we'd painted the room a pale shade of pink like an opal. We were taking a chance like we did when we painted our kitchen blue. But the color lit up the room, pulling everything together, making the room seem sunny during the day and cozy at night. Even Juniper, a mere ball of soft black fur, seemed to fit into the color scheme.

"I thought that Tyler had a good vibe, that he liked me for who I am, that he would cherish me like you said I should cherish myself."

"You made a mistake. Tyler Chase was nothing like that.

He was a selfish, vain man who used you and was probably using Mona."

Tanya didn't say anything for a moment, maybe thinking about what I'd just said.

"Do you remember when I told you about my Pa Nettie?" she asked after a sip of tea, lost perhaps in thoughts of her past both recent and distant as I had been.

"I remember you said you loved him very much, and that he raised you after your mother died."

"After my grandma died," she corrected me. "Nana raised me after my mother died. Pa Nettie was Nana's longtime boyfriend. He still drank a lot when I came to live with him but tried to stop, and I loved him for that. Pa Nettie looked out for me more than anybody else did. Pa Nettie was black like I think my father was. My mother's people, except for Nana, were real prejudiced, and they didn't want me or her in their life. Bad luck seems to have followed me from the day I was born," she said with a chuckle we both knew wasn't one.

"But you had your grandmother before she died and Pa Nettie. That was good luck, right? You said nobody cherished you? Pa Nettie cherished you. He looked out for you as long as he could. He was a blessing, and I know you were a blessing to him. You have a lot of blessings, Tanya. You have your own business, right? You have—"

"Just leave me alone, Dessa! I don't feel like I am blessed and that's what counts," she said, her voice short and irritable. I stopped because she was right, and let her be. Maybe she needed more time to feel sorry for herself; we all do from time to time. When she spoke again, she whispered as if afraid someone was listening.

"Did you tell anybody about what happened last Saturday, like Harley or Vinton with his big mouth?"

"No, of course not."

"I don't want anyone to know. That was the most embarrassing thing that's ever happened to me in my whole life. I felt like a fool."

"It was on them, not you."

"I didn't mean it, what I said, that I wished they were dead; you know that, right?"

"You were angry and hurt. I knew you didn't mean it. But what do they think happened to him? You said his place was on fire; did he burn to death?"

She shook her head, slowly, as if still trying to figure things out before she spoke. "You know when you said that stuff about him living by the sword and dying by the sword? I think that's what happened to him, that somebody killed him with one of his swords or knives he was so proud of. All somebody had to do was snatch it off the wall."

I nodded because for all I knew she could have had it right.

"Why did you say that stuff anyway, about living and dying by the sword?"

The gift had prompted those words to tumble out of my mouth, but I wasn't about to bring that into the conversation. "It's just a saying, Tanya, that's all."

She waited a good minute before she spoke again. "You know what I think? I think Mona killed him. I think she killed her husband, and he knew it so she had to kill him, too. I think that baby is his, not Casey Osborne's. Don't ask me how I know, but I do and she might have killed him because of that. Do you think she might kill me, too?" she quickly added, her eyes wider than usual.

"That's a lot of thinking, Tanya, and not a lot of facts."

She stiffened, drew in a breath. "What if she tries to kill me?"

"I don't think you're in any danger, and I don't know if she killed her husband or Tyler. They were on very good terms when we left them." Tanya cringed as if she'd been slapped. "Because they were together doesn't mean they killed her husband," I said, trying a gentler explanation. "And the police already arrested somebody for Osborne's murder, and we don't know how Tyler died. He might have left a candle burning or a cigarette. Harley said something scary about him when he came into the office that day. I didn't tell you, but maybe I should have. He said that Tyler had connections with guys you didn't want to cross. Maybe he was into dangerous stuff that nobody knew about. Maybe he double-crossed somebody and they got even. Unless you have real facts, something you can take to the cops, it doesn't do any good just to 'think' about what could have happened. You're letting your imagination run away with you."

"But maybe Red didn't kill him and whoever did is still out there."

Juniper chose this moment to sidle into the living room again, eager for a pat and treats. He gazed up at Tanya, then licked her hand, as if hoping that she might do his bidding. She laughed, lightly patting his head.

"He really likes me, huh," she said.

"He likes anyone who he thinks will give him a treat. I'll get some for you." I went into the kitchen, but my thoughts were on what Tanya had said about Tyler until I remembered that last piece of advice Aunt Phoenix had given me when she saw me yesterday: *Let things lie as they fall. Mind your own business. Don't look for trouble. Stay out of harm's way. . . . People aren't always what they seem.*

Stay out of harm's way. I couldn't remember the last time my aunt had been so forthcoming with a warning. Maybe she knew something she wasn't yet ready to tell me. Or maybe not. I checked my cell phone just in case, but there was no text waiting. But what were those words if they weren't a warning? Maybe simple advice that I should listen to. Unless I knew something the cops didn't know, it would do no one any good to pay too much attention to what Lacey or Tanya had said. *Mind your own business.*

And just what was the meaning of this blasted silver streak running down the side of my face?

I returned to the living room with a bag of salmon Temptations, Juniper's favorite, for Tanya, and she let him nibble some out of her palm. She giggled again, offering a glimpse of the little girl who had lost her childhood.

"Pa Nettie had a black cat like this except that he had a white patch on his chest," she said after a minute. "He was skinny, and mean, but he loved me and Pa Nettie and I loved him. He ran away after Pa Nettie died. Do you think cats come back, like reborn in another body? Maybe this is Pa Nettie's cat who has come back. His name was Nubbie."

As if on cue, Juniper snuggled up to her again, hoping for more treats. "No, Juniper is a ham," I said.

"Are you telling me that a cat can come back as a piece of meat?" Tanya said, looking perplexed.

"You're a soft touch, Tanya, and he senses that," I said, unprepared to discuss the concept of reincarnation, but it was also the truth. "Sometimes beings, even greedy little cats, take advantage of people with generous hearts."

"I don't have a generous heart."

"I think you do," I said, remembering the vulnerability of that soft glimmer that had struck me the night she was crying in the car.

"They really took advantage of me, Mona and Tyler. I should have known from before who they were. You know like that famous old saying says, about believing people the first time they tell you who they are. I think it's definitely true."

"Yeah, it's from Maya Angelou." Thanks to Aunt Phoenix, I knew my quotes well.

"Who?"

"Did you just say that you knew Mona and Tyler from before?" I said, unwilling to take the time to enlighten her, but I also recalled what Louella had said about those old days. They were all around the same age and must have known each other as kids.

"A long time ago. We were in high school then. Before Charlie and all the crap we did and all of that. When we were pure and innocent."

"Pure and innocent?"

She gave a sly smile. "Kind of."

"Did you know that Mona's sister, Millie, killed herself?"

She shook her head. "That must have happened when we were little kids. Like in kindergarten. I knew them in high school."

"What were they like then, Mona and Tyler?"

"Mona was always high-class, turned up her nose at kids like me and Louella, and I always hated her because of that. She got anything she wanted. Her mom was always there for her. Her daddy was rich, too, so she had nice clothes. I kept hoping something bad would happen to her, serve her right, but it never did."

"It's happened to her now. She just lost her husband."

"Like she really cared about him. It makes sense Mona would end up with a rich dude like Casey Osborne even though he was old as dirt."

"Not that old," I said. "He was only a couple of years older than me."

"Well, you know what I mean. Older than her and Tyler."

"How about Tyler, what was he like?"

"He was a jock. Fencing isn't football but he was into sports and a state champion and people liked him because he was good-looking and that made up for him not having any money. He and Red were friends but hung out with some hardheads. They were cool until Tyler started making moves on Louella. She didn't mind because if there's anything that girl likes it's attention. But Red kicked his butt. *Seriously* kicked his butt."

"So Red can get violent?"

"Just 'cause you kick somebody's butt doesn't mean you're violent," she said, and chuckled lightly. "It was kind of cool in a way if you know what I mean. You always feel protected with a man like that, who will beat somebody up if he messes with you."

"Until he turns that temper on you and beats you up, too."

"You just need to know how to control men like that. And Louella knows how to control him."

I thought about Charlie Risko, whose temper had turned on her so many times she'd had to wear turtlenecks to conceal her bruises. Had Tanya really forgotten that?

"And you knew how to control Charlie Risko?" The look that came on her face made me wish I hadn't said it. Those wounds were still fresh, and she didn't need reminding. She dropped her head without answering.

"Is Red like Charlie Risko?" If he was, I had to find a way to get Louella away from him. I remembered her mother's words about Louella's grandfather. Bertie's unhealed wounds from his abuse led to who she became.

Tanya shook her head. "Red isn't Charlie Risko. Nobody could be like Charlie was, and that's why somebody killed him," she said, her voice subdued.

The room seemed to darken, as if conjuring up the memory of Tanya's late husband had snuffed out the sun; either that or the gift was reminding me of his presence. We sat for a while silently sipping our coffee and tea.

"I've got to get home. I've got stuff to do," Tanya said abruptly as if something important had just occurred to her. "Don't worry about Louella; she can take care of herself. Red's liable to beat somebody up, but only if he or she is threatening Louella or his daughter. He wouldn't hurt either of them."

Tanya stroked Juniper's back a few times, picking him up to plant a kiss on his nose. Ever the beggar, Juniper lifted his head and purred. "Thanks for the tea, and stuff," she said, giving the cat another pat. "Let me know if you need some help dyeing that gray. It makes you look old."

"Are you sure about Red?" I asked, ignoring her offer and still uneasy.

"How well does anybody really know anybody? Look what happened to me with Mona and Tyler. No way I could have guessed they would do that. I thought he was really into me. He acted like he was, giving me his key and everything."

I sipped my coffee without expression or comment.

"I don't understand why you are so worried about Red. Isn't he still locked up somewhere?" Tanya said, then, blowing me a kiss, she left quickly with the lazy little shrug that so often defined her, the unanswered question lingering in the air.

Chapter 11

I went back upstairs when Tanya left to take another look at my overnight streak. It was as puzzling now as it was the first time it happened, but then I had Darryl to give me a hug and a boost of confidence. I was on my own now. I tried hiding it underneath a colorful head wrap, snatched it off, then tried a silk headband, but the hair kept slipping out. Apparently, it was there for a reason and it was a waste of time to try to hide it. I'd ask my aunt about it on Sunday; it was within her purview, one of those peculiarities that marked my life as a "gifted" woman that she would need to explain. In the meantime, I'd just live with it as I always did until I got sick enough to dye it again. I had another cup of coffee, looked in the refrigerator for a snack to munch on, then decided to head to that place I go when I'm out of sorts, need cheering up or something good to eat.

It was going on noon when I got to Royal's Regal Barbecue, just in time for lunch. Georgia, Lennox's faithful counter woman and assistant cook, was at the counter serving customers. Without a word or smile, she nodded toward the dining room, indicating she knew why I was here. Lennox was sitting with his daughter, Lena, at her table in the back where she listens to her iPhone or sculpts clay; it was clay today. Sometimes he plays with her, doing whatever she does, shuffling cards or trying his hand at drawing or sculpting, which makes her laugh at his ineptitude. More often he simply watches her, smiling when she does, simply happy to be close.

I sat at a distant table not wanting to interrupt. Lennox had told me more than once that his daughter made him a better man, more patient with himself and life, more aware of things most people took for granted. She had changed him in ways that nothing else could, and he owed her his life. I'd wondered what he meant when he said that but understood it now; the depth of his love for his daughter was palpable.

Tanya's lack of love still haunted her. Pa Nettie had been the one steady person in her life, but he'd been a drinker, and although he'd tried to stop, he hadn't. Like any child raised by alcoholics, it affected her in ways she didn't fully understand. Her bad luck with men may have had as much to do with her childhood as anything else. It wasn't hard to imagine why she'd be jealous of Mona Osborne, who seemed to have all the breaks. Tanya's assumption that she had murdered her husband, and even Tyler Chase, was probably based on envy. Yet Lacey harbored the same suspicion—and so had I.

I wanted to find out more about Tyler Chase's death. Tanya only knew what she'd heard on TV, and I was curious about exactly how he'd died. Lennox Royal wasn't a cop anymore, but he still had friends on the police force and more than likely they shared what was happening in town with him.

Lena noticed me first and broke out in a wide smile. "What happened to your hair?"

"It does that sometimes, turns a different color on me. What do you think I should do?"

"Pink! Will you dye it pink?"

Lennox Royal glanced at me and grinned. "Looks great to me, Dessa. Leave it like it is. Gives you a mysterious edge."

"You don't know the half of it," I said, turning back to Lena. "If I decide to dye it, I'll definitely consider pink. Have you ever heard of a chocolate chip cookie cake? I'm going to make one just for you and bring it by." Her smile broadened, which I didn't think possible; then she went back to her clay.

Lennox kissed her forehead and joined me at my table. "So how long have you been sitting here? I was so busy hanging out with Lena, I didn't see you come in. Want something to eat?"

On cue, my stomach growled audibly, so there was no use in lying. "Well, I did miss breakfast, but I don't want you to go to any trouble. I actually dropped by to talk about something else. By the way, I'm serious about that chocolate chip cookie cake for Lena. You might like it, too."

"No thanks. Sounds like a chocolate martini. Give me my stuff straight. Don't want chocolate chips messing up a cake." I chuckled because that had also been my reaction. We sat at one of the smaller square tables, easy in each other's presence. It was getting like that between us, comfortable, which always took me by surprise. I wondered if he felt the same way.

"Sure you don't want anything to eat? I *know* you're hungry. Come on, Dessa. Cooking is my raison d'être. Didn't think I knew French, did you? Let me make you a sandwich. Something to hold you until dinner."

Before I could refuse, he rushed into the kitchen and came back with a tuna on rye and two Cokes. "Not everybody who comes here for lunch wants barbecue. There are such fools! I always keep a good supply of tuna and chicken salad."

I gobbled down one half of the sandwich, then the other.

"Want another?" He didn't hide his amusement.

I shook my head, embarrassed by how quickly I'd wolfed them down. He watched me, still amused, and took a sip of Coke. "So what do you want to talk to me about? Let me guess. The guy who was found dead in his town house the other day. You knew him, right?" He peered at me from across the table with a slightly raised eyebrow.

"Well, kind of."

"Connected to that crew you work with, right?"

"Indirectly." I avoided his eyes, recalling our last conversation about the coincidence of violent crime linked to Risko Realty.

Lennox shook his head, slowly and deliberately. "Odessa, I'm worried about you." He meant business because he'd called me by my full name.

"I don't want to hear it!" I held up my hand in front of my face as if to stop his words. "Sorry, didn't mean to snap."

"No need to apologize." He took another sip of his Coke. "I should have known better. One thing I learned long time ago was not to talk trash about somebody's family, and I know that family is what you consider these folks."

"Yeah, but not Tyler Chase," I added quickly. "There was nothing family about that guy."

"How was he tied in?"

"Tanya, Charlie Risko's widow, was spending time with him. As things turned out, he was also seeing Mona Osborne, widow of the recently departed Casey Osborne."

"Brotherman has a thing for rich young widows. Not a good sign."

He picked up a folded newspaper left on the table with a photograph of Chase on the front page and skimmed it.

"According to this, he was Osborne's partner, which could make him a suspect in his death. But not necessarily. Chase was seeing both ladies?"

"*Seeing* is a polite way to put it. It's a sad story that's not mine to tell," I said, remembering my promise to Tanya about sharing her humiliation. "Have you heard anything about the way he died? There was a fire in his town house, but do you think that was what killed him?"

Lennox shook his head. "Far too soon to tell. Just because a burned body is found in a fire doesn't mean fire caused the death. That has to be determined by the medical examiner and fire investigator working together to see and analyze the evidence. It can be done but takes a while."

"When will they know?"

"It's hard to say. They need to establish the timeline leading up to the fire as well as time of death. They have to determine where the body was found, the burn patterns on his clothing, the room, his body, where the fire originated. There are ways they can determine if he died before the fire was lit, but that will take time if the body was charred. If they know that, they still need to find out how he was killed. Was he murdered or did he fall asleep holding a cigarette? Did he smoke? Did he burn candles? Most accidental fires happen when somebody gets drunk and falls asleep holding a cigarette or forgets to blow out a candle."

"He smoked," I said, remembering the ashtrays filled with cigarette butts. "And he wasn't the neatest guy in the world and he did burn candles."

"How do you know all that?" Curiosity sparked in his eyes.

"That's part of the story that's not mine to tell."

Lennox didn't hide his bewilderment but gave me the better part of a doubt. "Fire investigations are something I don't know much about except it would take more than two or three days to determine exactly what happened. So you think the widow, the recent one, had something to do with his death?"

"I don't know, but do you think Tyler Chase could have been involved in Casey Osborne's death?"

"I doubt it. Give the cops some credit. He and the widow would have been first on the list, especially if the police suspected they were lovers. An unfaithful wife is always someone they put under serious consideration. But they didn't arrest either of them, so they must know things we don't, either about their relationship or alibis."

"Neither of them was there when he died."

"That's one thing."

"But the police pinned it on Red too quick. He was convenient, has a record and motive. Besides that, Mona Osborne was the grieving wife, pretty, rich, and very pregnant. Not your typical murder suspect."

Lennox sipped the rest of his soda and rocked back in his chair. "I'll give you that. Cops are like everybody else, with their own biases and prejudices that get them in trouble, stand in the way of them doing their job. It was the reason I left the force and retired like I did. I didn't like what I was seeing." He stopped short without saying anything else, which whetted my curiosity, reminding me how little I really knew about this man's past life. I'd assumed he'd left the police force to take care of his daughter, but that must not be the whole truth. "Another story, another day," he said, noting my expression. "Let's get back to your murders if that's what they really are."

"You don't think they could be connected?"

"I doubt it. Different methods. Osborne was poisoned, right, or so they say at this point, even though they haven't really determined that, even though they arrested somebody for it. Chase died in a fire, until other things, yet unknown, are determined. You follow facts as they present themselves, and those are the facts you have. Making assumptions always gets you in trouble."

He leaned back in his chair, though, as if considering something that hadn't occurred to him before. "One thing has always bothered me about how quickly they jumped on Avon Bailey, Red as you call him. If he poisoned the guy, what kind of poison did he use and how did he get him to take it?"

"You said before that you thought Louella might be his accomplice. That maybe she had made it possible for Red to get into the house and to give it to him," I said, recalling the first conversation we'd had about Osborne's death. "But she'd never been in that house before either, not before she went there with me. I know that people lie, but she's not a liar; I'm sure of that."

"How are you so sure?"

"I have my ways," I said, playing up the "mysterious" aspect of my new look.

Lennox smiled. "Okay, I'll give you that, but why are you so certain that Red and she are innocent?"

"Because I know Louella and because of something that Osborne's son, Lacey, said."

"Osborne's son?"

"Yeah, he's a teenager, about fifteen."

"Who the hell names a boy Lacey?" Lennox said more to himself than me. "But who the hell names a boy Lennox, for that matter?" he added with a self-conscious chuckle. "Tell me what he said."

"Lacey stopped by my house the other day to drop something off. I heard him say that he believed his stepmother, Mona, might be responsible for his father's death."

"Told you that out of the blue?"

"No, actually, I overheard him tell another child who was visiting me. But he was convinced."

Lennox paused, considering what I'd said. "He may have been trying to impress the other kid. Children do that sometimes. Break bad to make themselves seem tough."

"Not in this case. He was talking to Erika, Red's young daughter, and explaining to her why he knew her father wasn't responsible for the murder of his."

Lennox whistled long and low. "That's a heavy conversation for two kids to have. What exactly did he say?"

"Just what I said, that he knew who killed his father, and it wasn't Red."

"Did he say how he knew?"

"No, just that he needed to get some proof."

Lennox scowled, a rare expression for him, as if the thought that crossed my mind had just crossed his. "What do you know about this kid?" His tone suggesting that he was wondering about this "proof" Lacey might be setting out to get. "Is he what they call a troubled child?"

I thought back to what one of the ladies in the Aging Readers Club had said about Lacey's fascination with swords and that he was "a bit troubled," as she cautiously put it. "He likes books about swords. That's all I know for sure," I said, not mentioning what I knew about Tyler Chase's fascination but wondering if that could be connected to Lacey.

"Hell, I liked reading about swords and King Arthur and the Knights of the Round Table when I was a kid. I loved chess, too, almost as much as basketball. My grandfather taught me how to play, and I only beat him once, right before he was getting ready to die." He paused just long enough to tell me there was more to that story and his life than he was ready to share. There was much about this man that I didn't yet know and wanted to. "Some folks might think that was weird for a black boy growing up like I did to love chess and the Knights of the Round Table, but not all kids are predictable. Now if you told me the kid was hurting small animals and setting fires, that would be a problem."

I didn't mention what the ladies had reluctantly shared about the fires in the school, but I couldn't forget what they'd said, nor Lacey's reaction to Juniper, even though Juniper had been the aggressor, not the other way around. Could fear like that lead to cruelty? I suspected that it could.

"Troubled kids usually find ways to show their anger. Cutting their bodies, missing school, acting out, always sad.

They take things out on themselves by finding ways to get attention, usually negative, if that will make people show that they care about them."

If there was ever a kid who needed attention it was Lacey Osborne. I just didn't know how far he'd go to get it.

"Does this Lacey kid fit that description? You better let the police know if he does."

"I don't think so. He's just an angry, grieving boy."

"Just out of curiosity, how does he think his stepmother killed his father?"

"Poison. Mona Osborne used to be a chemist. His mother says that's how they met. Casey Osborne was trying to acquire her company."

"Isn't that how the police think Red Bailey killed Osborne? That's probably where the kid got the idea. The God's truth is poison can be an explanation for lots of deaths because it is easier to get than you think. It can be in anything and everything. Too much aspirin or alcohol can take you out. Plants like lily of the valley and tansy. Castor bean seeds, potato sprouts—"

"Sprouts? Like in the eyes of a potato?"

"Potato sprouts contain solanine, a neurotoxin. You can extract it or grind it up and dry it. Don't forget cassava, if it's not cooked properly.

"I haven't even mentioned things like potassium chloride, a dead ringer for salt—the final stroke in a lethal execution. People use it in water softeners. Aconite is a root found in some herbal medicines, and if it is not processed properly and used in a tincture and added to a drink you can't taste it. The perfect poison. Don't forget old-school arsenic, in everything from seafood to rice. Or thallium, which is colorless, odorless, tasteless—but it's hard to get unless you have connections. The list goes on and on.

"The kid doesn't know this, but you wouldn't need to be a

chemist to figure out how to poison somebody. Anyone could do it, including Red. Thallium and arsenic are both used in rat poison, which is probably why the cops settled on Red, who had access to both."

We sat for a time not saying much, me wondering if maybe the boy was on to something but not sure what. Lennox, the cautious detective, keeping his thoughts to himself. When my phone vibrated I quickly checked it, expecting a text from Aunt Phoenix, but it was Louella:

Need help. NOW!

I texted her back, then called, but got no answer.

"Time for me to get back in that kitchen and get ready to feed some hungry folks," Lennox said, with the grin that always seemed to come when he talked about cooking. "You want to stick around?"

"No, I better go." I was concerned about the tone of Louella's text.

"Come back soon. I need to talk to you about . . . something else . . ." he said with a nod toward Georgia, who gazed at us from the open kitchen door.

I nodded as if I was listening to him, but I wasn't. Louella's words had raised the hairs on the back of my neck.

Chapter 12

I rang her bell twice, but it wasn't Louella who opened the door.

"Red?" I asked even though I knew it must be him, but he wasn't wearing an ankle restraint. Had they cut him loose or had he found a way to get it off like desperate people do?

"They let me out," he said, answering the question I didn't ask.

"I noticed." I said it casually, lessening the tension filling the space between us, but I was uneasy. It had only been a few weeks, but he'd lost weight since I'd last seen him fighting and cursing on the Osborne kitchen floor. He was still a big guy, his bulky frame nearly blocking the narrow doorway. It was clear to me now that he'd been arrested so quickly because he was a hefty black man with a record, fair game for somebody looking for a suspect.

"You're Dessa the caterer, right? Louella's friend. Did she tell you what happened?"

"No, she texted me, just told me to come by." I didn't mention her needing me or the *NOW!* in caps. I didn't know what was going on between them, what had happened, or what to make of him, but I was worried about Louella. "So where is she?" I said as casually as I could.

"Out."

"Out where?" I tried to take the note of alarm out of my voice but fell short. He looked surprised but tried not to show it.

"I don't know. She didn't say. Just said she was going out for a while. Took Erika with her."

"Is she okay?" I watched him for any sign, glimmer or anything else, that might tell me who he was, what he was hiding.

"What do you mean, is she okay?" He was offended and didn't care if I knew it.

"Just what I said, is she okay?" I'm nobody's idea of tough, willing to stand up to somebody twice my size. I was surprised to hear that quality in my voice, but that's what came out.

Red cocked his head, as if trying to figure me out, then gave up. "I surprised them, showing up like I did. Kind of showed up out of the blue, and she left."

"What do you mean, you showed up out of the blue?" I sounded like an interrogator, and he took a breath before answering, his words slow and measured, as if sick of explaining himself to someone he knew wouldn't believe him.

"I didn't do it, and they know that now. They did an autopsy on the man, and say he probably died of a heart attack or fit, some kind of natural cause that didn't have anything to do with me. I didn't poison him with rat poison or anything else. I laid low for a couple of days until I could get myself together enough to come over here this morning to see my kid." He paused then, his eyes locking on to mine. "So you want to come in and wait for them here or are you scared of the big bad murderer?"

His words took me aback. "Sorry, I didn't mean to sound like a cop."

"I'm used to it," he said in a tone that saddened me. "Come

on in if you want or come back later. Whatever you do is okay with me."

I followed him into the all-too-familiar living room where I'd sat less than two weeks ago listening to Louella, scared about his fate, and Erika, worried about what had happened to him. He lit a cigarette, took a few long drags, then snuffed it out. "Got to get rid of this before the warden gets home," he said with a hint of a smile. "The kid watches me like a hawk. She's scared cigarettes are going to take me out. Don't have the heart to tell her that cigarettes are the last thing that are going to be the end of her old man. Got a lot more to worry about than Marlboro Lights."

"The warden being Erika."

He laughed deep in his throat, more guffaw than chuckle. "Yeah, she watches us both, me and Louella. She's got high expectations, higher than I think we have for ourselves. We need to learn to live up to her standards, especially me. I want to be the best daddy I can, not like my father was to me. Not like him."

We sat stiffly and awkwardly on opposite sides of the room, me on the couch they'd tried to make new, Red squeezed uncomfortably into a secondhand armchair. He lit another cigarette, snuffed it out again, then went into the kitchen and came back with a can of rose-scented air freshener, spraying it around until the room was filled with the scent of fake roses. "You still smell it? The cigarettes, I mean."

I shook my head, but he cracked the window anyway, a good thing.

"They didn't have nothing on me, so they had to let me go," he said, repeating in different words what he'd already told me.

"When did you get out?"

"Wednesday." A thought came and left that I tried to ignore but got stuck. Tyler Chase was dead and it would be days before anyone knew exactly what happened. There was Red's temper and Louella's questions about who had told the cops about it and why. There had been bad blood between them when they were young. Even though Harley hinted that Tyler knew men who would sooner cut your throat than say hello, there were no facts about that. Yet there were two things I knew for sure: Red was out of jail. Tyler Chase was dead. I shifted uncomfortably on the couch.

"Did you know Tyler Chase?" I asked, the words tumbling out of my mouth like they sometimes do before I think about them good. Red shifted in his chair, eyes grown cold and glazed with mild contempt.

"Why are you asking me something like that?"

"You know he's dead, right?"

"Louella told me when I got home this morning. Said she heard it on the news. You think I had something to do with that, too. Is that what you think, that I got out of jail and somehow got over to where he lived and killed him, too?"

I drew back, further unsettled by his anger.

He shook his head in what looked like disgust. "Look, I didn't mean to yell at you, but according to the cops, everybody in this whole damn town knows I have a temper and thinks I'm capable of killing somebody in cold blood. Folks assume I'm hateful, just like my old man. Yeah, I know Chase is probably the one who told the cops I had a problem with Osborne. I don't know why he would tell them that, but most likely he did. He knew where I worked, too, because he was there with Osborne's wife, Mona, when I came looking for Osborne."

Anger shone in his eyes, Erika's eyes. "I'm glad that bastard is dead. Let me make that plural. Glad they both got what they deserved, however the hell they got it." He lit another cigarette, forgetting his pledge to his daughter. I noticed a glimmer, grayish purple, settling over him, lingering, then disappearing. Or was it simply cigarette smoke circling his head?

"Why are you looking at me so hard?" he asked.

"I thought I saw something."

"What?"

"Nothing important."

"Do you really think I could do something like that?" he said, glaring at me hard, but despite his anger I noticed how sad and filled with shame his eyes were. Erika's eyes turned grown and sorrowful.

"I don't know you, but to tell the truth you don't strike me as that kind of man," I said, taking a chance with honesty. The grayish glimmer had faded into a pale pinkish one. I admitted to myself that up until this moment I'd been afraid of this man and I wasn't anymore. My thoughts suddenly turned to Lena, laughing with her father telling me to dye my silver streak pink, just like this glimmer had done switching from gray to pink. Probably some kind of craziness courtesy of the gift playing its tricks. Another question for my aunt when I saw her. Despite my annoyance, though, I found myself smiling, a slight hesitant smile, because in that moment, with or without that temper, I knew this man, as menacing as some people thought he might be, wouldn't harm anybody in this world, least of all me.

"My aunt Betty had dimples like yours. I been partial to dimples all my life," Red said, a sheepish smile pushing its way to his lips, brought up by the memory of somebody he loved.

"Your smile is nice, too, if you'd let it be," I said, which broadened it. He let out a breath, slow and easy, as if he'd been holding it in for a long time. It was then that he began to talk tentatively, as if he wasn't sure he wanted to speak.

"You know what you saw that day, that man doing all that

cursing and yelling, rolling around on the floor with Harley at that party, that wasn't me. It was somebody who comes out every now and then, when I don't want to see him. Somebody who was part of my father that I hated. I don't want to be that dude, but that's who I am sometimes."

I tried to remember everything Harley had told me about Red's father, but it was more than a year ago and too much had happened since then. I recalled him saying that Avon Bailey, Red's father, had been a cruel man. Louella had said that Red didn't use his full name because he didn't want to share it with the father he hated.

"What was your father like?" I asked even though I knew.

"Mean, violent with a temper like I said. That's why I did what I did to him. I couldn't kill him, so I did the next best thing. Took his money."

I let that linger, then told him what I knew. "You and Louella were both involved with Charlie Risko back in those days when he was stealing people's property, weren't you?"

"Yeah."

"You know that Charlie Risko was the man who stole your father's houses, not Casey Osborne. He was just the one who bought the land they were on."

His face went blank, then hard, and he couldn't look me in the eye. Maybe guilt still haunted him for the part he'd played in stealing his father's land, depriving himself of his own birthright.

"I know who stole it. I know what I did, and I've paid for it good; so has Louella. And Charlie Risko is dead, and that's good, too. But that's in the past. My past. You know how much that property is worth now? More money than you can imagine. Charlie Risko didn't know what he was doing when he wrote up those deeds and papers. He wasn't a lawyer, just a crook. He didn't do it right. That land he sold to Osborne didn't really belong to him. It still belonged to my father."

"How do you know?"

"When I got back home running from myself and spending time locked up down south, I heard my daddy was dead. Before he died, he was looking for me all over town, even went to the police, filed a report, but I didn't want to be found; I'd disappeared. I didn't want to see him or anybody else again. But then I started feeling maybe I should pay my respects to him, he was my daddy, after all, so I went by the nursing home where he spent his last days to find out where they buried him. They gave me the keys to a safety-deposit box that he'd left for me. When I opened it, I found a letter from him, legal papers, and a deed that proved what I just told you, and now I had the proof I needed."

"Did you tell Osborne?"

"Yeah, I went over to his house first thing, then twice more. I was polite the first time. Knew he was a businessman and would want to do the right thing. I didn't want it all, just what belonged to me. I told him Charlie Risko had swindled him the same way he did my daddy. Osborne said he'd look into it, but when I didn't hear from him, I knew he was probably getting ready to fight me in court."

"You had been to his house before he died?"

"Yeah. I just told you that."

"Louella said you'd never been there."

"I lied to her about it. I do that sometimes," he said, which made me wonder what other lies he had told.

Silence can be a healing thing, settling as it will within a space before it's filled with words. It can also make you doubt yourself, and I wondered as I sat here with Red if maybe I was wrong about him, if that pink glimmer I'd seen for that moment had been a mistake, had no meaning at all. If his comment about his aunt's dimples had blinded me for the half second it took to know who he was. Another trick from the ever-playful gift. I had no idea who this man really was. I'd have to wait for him to tell me, and finally, after some time had passed, he did.

"I need to leave my baby something for all that time I was gone. Give my daughter what my daddy never gave me, more than love, something concrete she can have, hold on to. I need to find a way to get back some of the property Charlie Risko and Casey Osborne stole so she can have it back, find a way to make me forgive myself for what I did."

"What did your lawyer say?"

"I was too broke to have one." He shook his head like he was ashamed or it had grown heavy on his shoulders. "That's where Tyler Chase comes into it. I called Chase because I knew him from when we were young, and he promised, actually swore, that he'd talk to Osborne, make him come to an agreement with me, because he knew I was right. The crazy part is I actually believed him, trusted him. But he never did, just told those cops what he wanted them to know, that I'd been there and had an ongoing fight with Osborne."

He looked up at me suddenly as if just remembering something. "You ever spend any time locked up? I don't need to ask you that, because I know the answer. You're not the kind of person who ends up doing stuff that will make people think you've lost your mind."

"You don't know me as well as you think," I said, considering the peculiarities that marked my life.

"You're not the kind of lady who would let something like that happen to you. Not unless you got involved with the wrong man, with a loser like me; that's what scares me about Louella. That's why I didn't come back right away, when they took off that ankle restraint. I worry about being in their lives, hurting them."

"As far as I know, they're glad you're here."

"You know what Bertie, Louella's mother, did. I don't want to bring anything else like that down on their heads. I love them both too much for that. When they let me out, I thought maybe they were better off without me. I'm still not sure if I made the right decision, if I'll stay. I'm here tonight, and I'll see how it goes. You think I should stay?" he asked, taking me by surprise.

"I really don't know and I'm not going to lie to you."

"Thanks for telling me what you really think."

"Just do right by them, that's all. Ask me again in a year, and I'll tell you the truth as I see it."

Neither of us spoke for a while, both of us considering what was said. Red seemed lost in his thoughts, which he wasn't about to share, and I didn't expect him to.

"You want something to drink? I mean like some tea," he said nervously, filling the awkward silence between us, maybe embarrassed by the truth as I told it. "That's all I can make, is tea. Unless you want a glass of milk or juice. I wish I could offer you coffee, but I don't know how to make it. All I drink is instant and she doesn't have any of that. Louella's got this fancy contraption, but I have no idea how to work it. Another reason I should probably get the heck out of here before Erika gets attached to me. I'm no good around here. Can't even make a damn cup of coffee!" He stood up, then sat back down, his shoulders slumped in humiliation.

"If that's actually a reason you might consider leaving, we can take care of that right now. Do you know how to boil water?"

He looked surprised but followed me into the kitchen. This was a chance for me to see another side of this man, his defenses down, no anger—simply a guy who wanted to learn something new so he could impress the woman he loved. As the water boiled, I showed him how to grind coffee beans, explaining that if they were too coarse the coffee would be weak and too fine it would be bitter. As we stood together in the small, modest kitchen he listened, genuinely interested in everything I had to say. I added the ground beans to the pot, four tablespoons for the sixteen-ounce carafe, stirred it slightly, then explained that we had to wait for four or five minutes before we plunged.

"I used to cook with my mom before she died," he said, a trace of sadness in his voice.

"This isn't really cooking," I said, but he was lost in his own memories and didn't hear me.

"I was a kid then."

I could still see the wounded little boy in his bearded face and knew that if I was lucky this might be a conversation between us for another day.

"That's how I knew I had a daughter, because Erika looked like my mom," he said, glancing up at me now.

"She looks like you. Some people say it's good luck to look like your father."

"You think so?" he asked, as if he was surprised.

"Yeah, I do," I said. "Actually, it's good luck to look like any parent who loves a child as much as you love yours."

When the coffee was brewed, we sat across from each other at the narrow kitchen table. He always drank his black, he said, and when I told him that was the mark of a true coffee lover he chuckled lightly as if he was proud of it. I poured milk in mine, a mistake because it was sour, but it really didn't matter.

And that was how Louella found us, chatting about nothing, drinking our coffee later in the day than was wise.

"You came! Thank God!" she said, plopping two bags of groceries down on the table.

"Daddy, you can't be in here; it's a surprise!" Erika grabbed Red's arm and pulled him, coffee cup still in hand, out of the kitchen before he could object.

I waited to make sure they were gone before I said anything to Louella. "What the heck is going on? Are you okay?"

"Of course I'm okay!" Louella said with a dreamy smile on her face as she sat down across from me in the spot Red had left. "Why did you think something was wrong?"

"That text, Louella! 'Need help. NOW!' *Now* in capital letters. How the heck did you think I was going to react? For all I knew, you were scared and in trouble!"

"How could I be in trouble? Red's here! I just meant I needed your help deciding what to cook for the surprise dinner," she stammered out, only slightly embarrassed.

"How come you didn't answer the phone or my text?" I said with obvious irritation.

"The store was crowded, I didn't have much money, and Erika was whining and getting on my nerves. I just didn't have time. I'm sorry. I didn't mean to worry you."

"Well, you did. But it doesn't matter now," I said, still annoyed, but deciding that it wasn't worth going into. Everything had changed for the best. "So what did you buy?"

"I wanted something special for Red's first dinner home with us after being by himself, and fried chicken is something you celebrate with. We all love Kentucky Fried Chicken, especially Erika, and I figured maybe mac and cheese and some green beans and apple pie to go along with it," she said, brimming with excitement.

As I went through her bag, I realized the girl had *definitely* needed my help. The mac and cheese was in a box; the green beans were in a can; the apple pie looked like it had been on the day-old shelf of a cheap supermarket. The chicken was just barely okay, and we'd need to work with it.

"Everything is good, right?" Her eyes begged for approval.

"It's always the spirit in which a meal is prepared that

counts," I said philosophically, and in this case, spirit was clearly what we'd be relying on. "Let's prep this chicken so we can fry it. Get out the oil and your frying pan and we'll get started."

Her blank expression told me she had neither frying pan nor cooking oil.

"Can you fry chicken in the oven?" she asked plaintively.

And here I was again, offering cooking lessons to another person in this young family who I seemed to be growing closer to by the day. I began with preheating the oven to 425 degrees F and issued a stern warning about the danger of getting salmonella poisoning from handling raw chicken and the importance of washing her hands before and after touching chicken. (All she would need would be for this family celebration to end up in the emergency room.) I showed her how to season the chicken with salt, pepper, garlic powder, and paprika—left over from God knows when—and shake a few pieces at a time in a bag filled with flour, and to make sure that every spot of it was covered. She called Erika to help with the shaking, who then proudly showed her mother that she knew how to measure a third of a cup of butter into a large pan.

We placed the pan in the oven to let the butter melt and sizzle but not brown. Then we put the chicken in to let it "fry" for fifty minutes, turning it once until it was done. By some stroke of luck, Louella found a meat thermometer left from the days of Bertie tucked away with other ancient utensils, which I promised to show her how to use another day. When we tested the temperature of the chicken and it had reached 165 degrees F we knew it was ready. Just to make sure, I cut into a thigh to be certain there were no traces of pink in the juice. It wasn't exactly Kentucky Fried, but if you were very hungry it was close enough.

When dinner was ready, the four of us sat around the

kitchen table. Erika bowed her head and said a prayer her grandmother had taught her and tears welled in my eyes as I thought about Bertie here in spirit, leaving the good she had within her along with the bad. I helped clean up, promising I'd come again and show Louella how to make a pie, and *real* mac and cheese. We watched a movie on the new TV they were both so proud of, and at Erika's request I took her upstairs, to tuck her into bed. We talked for a while before she went to sleep.

"You remember the kid who came by when we made the cookie cake?" she said.

"Lacey? Yeah, I remember."

"He must have found the proof he was looking for, because they let my daddy go. Would you thank him for me?"

"I will if I see him," I said, which was enough of an answer to put her mind at ease but, strangely enough, not mine.

When I lay in bed that night, I thought about what an exhausting yet strangely satisfying day it had been, from Tanya's tears to Erika's laughter, and I fell asleep with a smile on my lips. I woke up with a start at three in the morning. Folks call it the witching hour, that time of night when evil supposedly rears its head and runs ragged in the world. Somebody was in my driveway. I listened for a moment, decided it was nothing, and tried to go back to sleep. Something was moving the gravel. I picked up my cell to call the police, then hesitated, pulling up the shade to look outside first. It was Lacey Osborne riding his bike in circles. He stopped suddenly, stared up, then beckoned for me to come down to let him inside.

Chapter 13

"Lacey Osborne, what the heck are you doing in my driveway?" I yelled down from my window.

"Riding my bike," he said with that touch of sass teenage boys possess.

"I can see that! Does your mother know where you are?" I suspected that she didn't.

"No!"

"You need to call her."

"My cell is dead. Can I come inside?"

"No, I'll call her first."

"No! Please don't call her. Can I talk to you first? Please," he said, his voice cracking.

Despite all his sassy bravado, I realized he was crying. I could see that even from my upstairs window. Wondering if I should let him in, I watched him lean his bike on the side of the garage and walk around to the front door. He was a kid but a troubled one, his former teacher who knew about such things had said. I wondered what he had to say to me that he couldn't say to his mother. But I knew I couldn't just let him stand outside for the rest of the night. He'd come here for a reason. Still, I was hesitant.

He rang the bell three times, suddenly impatient. When I'm unsure of something, I consider what Darryl, always the better angel in my head, would do. He was always open to any kid who needed help and never turned down a child in trouble. If there was ever a boy who looked like he was in trouble and needed help it was Lacey Osborne.

"Where's your cat?" he said, hesitating before stepping inside. Juniper, always alert to the entrance of a stranger and the possibility of scoring Temptations, bounded down toward us from upstairs. Lacey uttered a gurgle of a scream and backed down the stairs, nearly tripping in his attempt to get away.

He may have been a troubled big kid, but he was still a kid.

I grabbed Juniper and carried him upstairs to the extra bedroom I use as an office. I filled one of his bowls with water, put food into the other, checked his litter, and placed him on the cat bed he never slept on. Firmly closing the door behind me, I headed back downstairs.

"Is he gone? I'm scared of cats," Lacey asked, apparently embarrassed.

"I know. I remember you told me that when you were here before."

"My dad said I should be ashamed of myself, being scared of cats, as big as I am, but I still am."

"Lots of people are scared of cats," I said, wanting to make him feel better. "Darryl, my husband, was scared of cats. He didn't own up to it, though, he just claimed he didn't like them, but I knew the truth. Then we got a cat and that cured him."

"How did it cure him?"

"Juniper is big now, but once upon a time, he was a cute little kitten with big ears and big feet, and they, he and Darryl, grew to be friends. Once you get to know what you're afraid of and understand it, you won't be afraid of it anymore."

He thought about that for a moment as if considering it.

"But I'm scared of other stuff, too." He leaned toward me as if somebody might be listening. "I'm scared a person I know is going to kill me. That's why I came over here, because I'm scared the person will find me. They won't find me if I'm here."

I didn't really believe that somebody was trying to kill the boy, but I couldn't chance it, so I peeked over his shoulder into my front yard, just in case. Nobody was there, the street empty and quiet. A dog was barking somewhere in the next block and a noisy cricket was in somebody's yard. It was spooky but not dangerously so. I stood aside so he could come inside, but I could see that he was trembling. He went to the couch and collapsed on it, as if he were carrying a backpack filled with rocks, then wrapped himself in the decorative cotton throw that lay across the armrest, snuggling into it like it was a cocoon.

"Who do you think is going to kill you?"

"I don't want to say."

"Then how do you know that this person, whoever it is, wants to kill you?"

He didn't answer but rather gazed around as if trying to get comfortable—or checking the whereabouts of Juniper.

"I just know! Can I have something to drink?" he said as if suddenly remembering he was thirsty.

"Sure, come into the kitchen. Are you hungry? I'll make you a sandwich."

"Okay, long as it doesn't have any nuts in it. I can't eat peanut butter and jelly or anything like that. I'm deathly allergic to nuts."

"I know. You told me that when you were here before, and your father told me, too."

"For real!" he said. The mention of his father seemed to energize him. He rose from the couch, followed me into the kitchen, and slid into a chair at the table. I'd picked up sliced turkey and American cheese from a deli a few days ago, and slapped together a messy sandwich on whole wheat bread and poured him a glass of orange juice.

He picked it up, studied it for a minute as if worried about the possibility of hidden nuts, and began to eat, voraciously. "Tell me what he said, my dad, about me being allergic to nuts. What did he say?" He talked fast between bites of the sandwich and gulps of orange juice, eating so fast I was afraid he might choke. "Tell me!" he said, glaring at me when he'd finished.

I recognized his interest for what it was; he was desperate to hear any last words his father had said, ones that he could always remember. I understood that desire only too well. I wished I had something more to tell him, something that he could treasure forever.

"When I met him, he told me that you were a very smart boy," I finally said, playing fast and loose with his late father's words. "He showed me your picture and he was very proud of you." I made him another sandwich and placed it in front of him. "I could tell how much he loved you.

"Sometimes it helps when someone you love is no longer with you to remember the good times you had, what you did together that made you both happy."

He picked the sandwich up, took a nibble, then placed it back on the plate as if reflecting on my words. "I liked hanging out with him, just sitting around with him in his office, studying what he did. He taught me how to play chess. I got to be real good at it and he liked that."

"My husband played chess, too." The memory of Darryl studying the board, his expression so intense and serious, came back sharp and sweet as it always did.

"Do you play, too?" Lacey asked, looking up.

"Not well. Darryl let me win sometimes, but I knew he was doing it."

"My dad did, too, let me win. He kept a board in his study. If we didn't finish a game, we'd leave it set up like it was and finish it later. When we played the next time, I'd have all my moves almost figured out. We were supposed to play that night, after . . ." He must have been uncomfortable sharing more, because he changed the subject. "So where is your husband? Does he live here?"

"No, he died a couple of years ago."

He paused for a moment, as if his breath had been knocked out and the mention of Darryl's death reminded him of his own loss, then stared hard at a calendar on a wall across the room. "If my dad hadn't had that dumb party he'd still be alive. I think about the last time I saw him, my dad. At that dumb party."

"You can't change something that has happened no matter how terrible it is." I told him the truth as I knew it even though nothing would lessen his pain.

"I was looking forward to staying at his house because we had a game to play and I was winning until . . ." He didn't finish. His thoughts must have turned to that day, the same as mine had. Osborne and Aurelia yelling at each other, pulling on him like two kids fighting over a doll. It saddened me that this was one of the last memories of his father the boy had. "I saw him the day before when I went over to play. I was glad because I knew my next move, and I had him fooled and I couldn't wait to move my knight," he continued, his voice shaking. "I brought him this stuff for his smoothie my mom made for me. But she must have been drunk when she made it. Before I drank it, she realized she'd accidentally added ground walnuts with the flaxseeds. I figured I'd surprise my dad, so I took it over to him to drink for breakfast the next day."

He finished the rest of his sandwich slowly as if his thoughts were lingering on that day, then drank the juice in two gulps.

"You don't believe me, do you?"

"About what?" I said, puzzled and not following him.

He saw my confusion and brought me back to where we'd begun.

"That I know somebody's trying to kill me because of what happened to my dad."

"If you want me to believe you, you have to tell me what you know."

He shook his head and yawned. "I'm going to lay down for a while, okay? My head hurts bad."

We went back into the living room, and he stretched out on the couch, closing his eyes. He was quiet for so long I thought he was asleep, but when I peeked over he was staring at the empty fireplace across from us. "You ever build fires in that thing?"

"In the winter when it's cold. I'm not that good at building them."

"I am." He closed his eyes, then spoke as if talking to himself. "I used to like to see them burn, fires. Not now, but when I was a kid I used to like it. That's how I know when I said before that somebody might be trying to kill me, because that person must know that about me, that when I was a kid I got in trouble for lighting fires, but I was just a kid then. I don't do that anymore."

"Glad to hear that," I said, trying to sound casual even though he'd just scared the heck out of me. I wondered why he was telling me this now and thought again about calling his mother. I sensed he trusted me, and I suspected that he was a kid who didn't trust easily. I couldn't betray that trust. Yet I had to make it clear that I wasn't going to allow him to play me and his mother against each other.

"Lacey, I need to call your mom and tell her where you are. I know she's worried."

"Don't call her, please. I don't want to go home now. She said she might not be home until late. I can't go there now." I heard fear in his voice, and I didn't know why.

"Okay, not right this minute, but I need you to tell me what's going on. You can't just say somebody is trying to kill you without saying why or who it is."

He nodded, reluctantly giving consent, then said, "You have any more of that cookie cake? That was good. Can I have some of that if you have any left?"

Had he lost track of time? That had been a few days ago. He wasn't dealing with reality, and that made me wary. "No, it's all gone, but do you remember the little girl who was here, Erika? I saw her earlier today and she wanted me to thank you for finding the proof that set her father free. Was it you who found it, that proof you told her you were looking for?"

He sat up so quickly he tossed the throw he'd wrapped himself in onto the floor. Covering his face with his hands, he began to tremble again. I sat down beside him and grabbed his hand for a moment, noticing how cold and sweaty it was before I let it go. Something or somebody had scared the heck out of this kid badly enough for him to show up here at 3:00 in the morning at the home of a woman he barely knew. I wondered if it had something to do with Tyler Chase's death, with when he had died and whatever had caused it. Lacey knew something. Did someone else know it, too?

"How long has it been since you were at home?"

"A while."

"Since when?"

"Since yesterday morning."

"Where did you go before you went home?"

"To talk to Tyler."

He avoided looking at me, and I wondered what he was hiding. "Did you see something at his place that you weren't supposed to see? Did you set that fire?" My questions were quick and bluntly asked, my concern disguised as best as I could, which wasn't enough, because he flinched. "Lacey, tell me what you saw and what you did?"

I had to lean close to hear him. "So like I told the little kid, I needed to find some proof. I went over there because I thought maybe I could find out if Mona or somebody else had something to do with my dad's death. That maybe Tyler knew something without realizing it. Tyler and me had a lot in common. I wanted to try out for the fencing team in school. He used to fence when he was a kid, and promised me when my dad was alive that he'd show us the awards he won as state champion and some of the fencing moves he knew. I knew that he was just trying to impress my dad, but that was okay because he was really loyal to him."

"When did you go?" He obviously knew nothing about Tyler and Mona's relationship.

"Yesterday afternoon. I kept ringing the doorbell. I was ready to leave when Tyler came outside. He had on pajama bottoms like he'd just gotten out of bed even though it was late, and he looked mad. I asked him if I could come inside and see the awards, and he grinned, like he was relieved. Said he was glad to see me."

"Did he let you inside?"

"No. He stood in the door like he didn't want me to see who was there. Do you think it could have been that lady who came with him to the party?"

I shrugged as if I didn't know, but of course I knew that it wasn't.

"He said he was honored that I remembered him considering all the stuff I'd been going through in the past few weeks. He said my dad was a special man and that he'd really cared about him and that he'd show me the awards like he'd promised. That he'd honor his word to my dad. He said that he'd added some new weapons to his display he wanted to show me."

"The sword display on his wall?"

"Yeah. I thought it was cool when I went over with my dad to visit him. I like that kind of stuff," he added, noticing the expression on my face. "You saw it?"

"Briefly," I said.

"He said he'd like to let me in, but it wasn't a good time because he was busy but to come by later that evening, and we could hang out. Said I was a good kid, said he was real sorry about what happened to my dad, but I shouldn't worry, because everything was going to be okay. Promised we would talk when I came back later."

"You went home then?"

He nodded. "Yeah, for a while. I told my mom I might go over later and she said it was okay so I went back over when I knew she was asleep. I started thinking about the things he used to say to me when my dad was around. How nice he'd been to me. I got hungry and stopped by a 7-Eleven to get some chips and a Coke, rode in the park for a while. I waited until it was late before I went back to Tyler's. I knew he'd fix me something to eat and let me spend the night on his couch if I waited long enough. He'd done that a couple of times before when I didn't want to go home."

He stopped talking, and the sigh when it finally came was from deep inside him and looked like it shook his whole body.

"I got to his place, and looked into his living room when I was on the front porch. His blinds were open, and he usually made sure they were closed. He and my dad used to joke about not wanting people to know what they were doing. Then I saw Tyler. He was lying on the floor in front of the couch. His hand was resting on the table like maybe he was trying to pull himself up, but he wasn't moving.

"I rang the bell, then tried to push the door open. It was so hot I couldn't touch it. I smelled smoke, too, coming from inside. I knew then that his place was on fire. I got really scared that he might be dead. I was going to call the fire department, then I thought they would think I set it because of what I used to do when I was a kid. It was so late I knew that nobody had probably been there but me and the person who set the fire, the one who might have hurt him. I got on my bike and rode away as fast as I could because I was afraid."

I was afraid for him, too. "You need to tell the police what you saw right away. You've been gone for a long time. I'm sure your mother has called them by now, and they might be looking for you. We need to tell her everything you saw so she can hire a lawyer to take you to the police so you can report it. The sooner they know what you saw and that Tyler may have been murdered, the closer they'll be to finding out who did it and the safer you'll be."

"But nobody knows where I am, so I'm safe here."

"For tonight, but that's all."

"Can we tell her in the morning? Can I sleep here? I don't want to go home now, please!"

I thought about it for a few moments, then nodded that it was okay. Whatever his reason, he wasn't yet ready to face his mother. Like most kids who have done something wrong, he was probably afraid she'd punish him for being out late or for not coming right home. I knew he had it wrong, but he'd been through enough already, and it wasn't a good time to argue with him one way or the other. Truth was, there were no lawyers to be had at 4:00 a.m. on a Sunday morning anyway.

I warmed up some milk and poured it into a mug, adding a generous dose of honey and a teaspoon of vanilla. He drank it slowly in tiny sips. When he finished, he lay down full length on the couch and fell asleep.

I watched him for a while like a nervous parent does a

child, even though he would be back with his mother as soon as possible. Aurelia could take it from there. I hoped she had the wisdom to hire a lawyer before she let him talk to the police. After Harley's and Red's experiences with the local cops, I knew a witness, even one as young as Lacey, could become a suspect in the blink of an eye, particularly when he was young, male, and black.

Sudden death certainly did seem to swirl around Mona Osborne, even though there was no proof she had anything to do with either man's demise. Osborne's was now considered due to natural causes. The reason for Chase's was undetermined, despite what Lacey saw or thought he did. Chances were, Mona might simply be as unlucky as Tanya Risko was when it came to losing men in tragic ways; you couldn't blame a woman for having bad luck with lovers. Yet there were coincidences that couldn't be ignored. Mona married the man who had caused the death of her older sister. She was a chemist with lethal knowledge of drugs, and most likely knew about her stepson's fire-setting past, but so did anyone close to him.

Yet this was not my problem to solve. Let the professionals worry about it. Aunt Phoenix's words came back to me then: *Mind your own business. Don't look for trouble. Stay out of harm's way.* Good advice worth following. Besides that, I was tired as heck. I watched Lacey for another minute, then headed upstairs. The day would be dawning soon, and I was sound asleep before the sun peeked into my window.

Chapter 14

The moment I woke up I knew that Lacey was gone. I don't know how I knew, but I did. It could have been the gift tossing out its occasional bounty or my intuitive sense about the unreliability of teenage boys. I ran downstairs anyway, two steps at a time, calling his name, hoping I was wrong. The throw he'd wrapped himself up in last night, because he was either chilly (always possible on a cool night) or scared, was neatly folded and laid across the armrest where it had been. I checked the kitchen, but the only traces were his empty mug, thoughtfully rinsed out and left to dry on the dish rack, and a note scribbled on a shopping list pinned by a magnet on my refrigerator: *Thank you for the milk and couch, Miss Dessa. I called my mom. I'm going home now.* I rushed outside hoping to spot him, looked up and down the street but was out of luck.

"Dessa, what are you doing out here so early on a Sunday morning?" said Julie Russell, my next-door neighbor, when she saw me. She was picking up her Sunday newspapers from her front porch, a big job for a little woman who weighed no more than one hundred pounds on any given day. She was a retired librarian; seemed like all my older acquaintances these days were either retired teachers or librarians—clearly, I'd missed my calling.

"Do you need some help?"

"No, but thanks. These Sunday editions do seem to get heavier by the week. I should read them on-line like most folks do, but I'm one of these old-fashioned ladies who like to turn the pages while I drink my morning coffee, despite the occasional ink smudge."

Like so many other things, her confessed love of newspapers reminded me of Darryl, which brought a sigh with a smile. "I was looking for a kid who spent the night on my couch. Have you seen a teenager on a bike riding down the street?"

"Yeah, as a matter of fact I did. I'm embarrassed to admit I thought it was the paper boy late with my papers, then remembered that kids don't deliver newspapers on their bikes anymore. That's definitely showing my age. Delivering newspapers is serious business these days, second or third job for some hard-working person trying to make ends meet. The boy was going somewhere fast. He spent the night on your couch? A relative?"

Occasionally, Julie could be overly curious, to put it kindly, about my business. It was a small fault and one I easily forgave. Her good intentions outweighed her prying manner. She was a thoughtful neighbor who was becoming a true friend.

"No, the child of a friend who is in trouble."

"You're taking him in?"

"No," I said more bluntly than I meant to.

She didn't seem offended. "Well, try not to worry. My years working with kids have taught me that they find their way home sooner or later, no matter how angry they are or how problematic that home is." She was trying to reassure me, but it didn't do much good; my expression must have shown it. "Oh, by the way, I love that silver hair. Very stylish. Very chic!" she added, an attempt to cheer me up.

"Thanks!" I forced a smile. I'd forgotten about the aberrant streak until she mentioned it.

"Don't worry," she said, hauling her papers inside. "If he's on his way home, he is probably fine."

I hoped she was right and that Lacey had told me the truth. I was beginning to feel guilty about not calling Aurelia when her son first walked through the door. He had been so adamant, though, so fearful about going home that I listened to him, following his lead. In the light of day, I wondered if it had been wise to heed the demands of a fifteen-year-old kid, especially one so traumatized he probably needed his mother's guidance. My good intentions might have been a serious mistake.

I dug through my handbag looking for the card on which Aurelia had scribbled her phone numbers. When I found it I texted her, then called and left a message asking her to get back to me as soon as she could. It was early and there was a chance she might not be awake. I left a message on her landline as well. I hoped she knew Lacey's story by now and had made plans to contact a lawyer on Monday morning, certainly before going to the police. At last, the boy was home where he belonged and that was good.

Yet I couldn't forget how Lacey had trembled, his whole body shuddering. You don't see that much, and when it's a kid, especially a boy who is big for his age and trying to be older, it leaves you undone. Most likely that fear that somebody wanted to kill him was imagined, yet he believed it. I knew enough about the vagaries of grief to appreciate that each person's experience is different and can't be predicted. Grief had to be lived through when it seemed impossible. Lacey had lost a parent, the worst thing that can happen to a child. He also believed his father's friend and partner had been murdered. After such trauma, it was understandable that a youngster might fear for his own life, even if that fear was imagined. The sooner Lacey was able to talk to the police and tell them all he knew the better—and safer—he would feel.

A screeching meow from the upstairs bedroom reminded me I'd forgotten an important member of my household, who was now feeling abandoned. I grabbed a couple of treats to soothe Juniper's impatience and ran upstairs to free him. His little green eyes flashed fiercely as he gobbled his treats. When I petted his head, I half expected him to rear back and nip at my hand, which he's been known to do when annoyed. But all seemed forgiven. He purred loudly, gave my hand a lick, and hightailed it downstairs to the kitchen for his breakfast.

After feeding my furry dependent, I made myself some coffee. Too lazy to grind beans, I tossed some Starbucks Veranda blend into the French press and poured in some hot water. Too impatient to let it "bloom," I pushed the plunger down and poured a lousy but well-deserved cup of coffee. The memory of Red and his rapt attention yesterday to the ins and outs of Louella's French press brought a smile. He was going to be all right; I was sure of that, at least for now. They all were. When my cell rang, I wondered if somehow my good thoughts had summoned Louella, then hoped it was Aurelia returning my call, but it was neither.

"Just wanted to remind you about the champagne. And make sure it's the good stuff," said Aunt Phoenix.

For one terrible moment, I didn't know what she was talking about; then I remembered. "Oh Lord!" I uttered without realizing I'd said it aloud.

"I know you didn't forget my birthday!"

"No, no . . . of course not!" I stammered even though she probably knew I was lying. So much had happened since I'd seen her that Friday it had completely slipped my mind.

"Well, I'm glad to hear that. Selma Wells is going to drop by for a toast, so make sure you bring real champagne. She's one of those women who will talk about you bad if you serve something cheap."

"Got it covered." Vinton, bless his heart, had bought me a bottle of Moët when I'd sold a house, and it had been sitting in the pantry for six months. I'd been waiting for the right opportunity to uncork it, and this was it. I put it in the refrigerator to get cold as we spoke. "You said something simple, right? Is a quiche okay?" There was no time to make anything else.

"Quiche?" She sounded disappointed.

"And we'll start with a first course. Tomato bisque. Homemade," I quickly added, using the term *bisque* loosely and with the guilty knowledge that *homemade* meant made from a can in my home. "You said simple, right?" I felt guilty because it was her birthday and I knew she wasn't crazy about eggs.

"That's fine. The main thing is that we're spending time together."

Aunt Phoenix was not one for sentiment. A pang shot through me. Was something happening with her health that she hadn't told me? What else would explain this birthday brunch coming out of nowhere? Despite my occasional annoyance with my aunt and the vague anxiety I often felt when I prepared to meet her, I loved her with every bit of my heart; the thought of something being wrong shook me to my core. Except for my aunt Celestine, whom I didn't know well, and legendary cousins, whom I wasn't eager to meet, she was all I had left of my family.

"Are you still there?" she asked.

"I am. I love you, Aunt Phoenix," I said, my voice catching.

"No need for all that! I'll see you soon enough, right?"

"Yeah. See you soon." I steadied my voice.

I took the quiche out of the freezer, prepping the rest of

the meal in my mind. I'd bake it when I got to her place so it would be warm when we ate it. I'd need to stop on the way to pick up sweet lettuce and arugula for a green salad. I'd shake up a quick balsamic vinaigrette while the quiche baked. A can of tomato soup could be nicely perked up with tomato paste, heavy cream, and fresh basil leaves with croutons to go on top, which were easy to do quickly with French bread swabbed with olive oil and baked in the oven. A sprinkle of parsley would be a final, colorful touch. I'd bring my own balsamic vinegar for the vinaigrette. I knew I could count on my aunt for good olive oil, which she claimed was a lifesaving staple, but she preferred apple cider to fancy vinegars, which in her mind included balsamic.

I went upstairs to dress, lamenting again the streak of silver hair running down the left side of my face. I tried tying my hair up with a head wrap again but couldn't wrap it properly. It was best to let it be since it was clearly some unwelcomed manifestation of the gift. My aunt would need to clear it up. I checked Juniper's water, gave him more food and a hug, then headed out.

I picked up most of the items I needed at an expensive fancy foodie market that had recently opened up, including some shortbread cookies in lieu of cake. I'd told my aunt I'd be there as soon as I could but hadn't said exactly when, which was a good thing. I assumed Lacey was safely home with his mother by now, but since I hadn't heard from Aurelia, I wanted to make sure everything was okay. When he told her that he spent the night on my couch, she'd probably want to know why I hadn't called her—with good reason. I owed her an explanation and it would have to be the truth, no matter how uncomfortable it made her.

Yet there was a nagging fear that Lacey hadn't gone home, that he'd kept on riding as fast as he could, as far as his bike would take him. If that was the case I was responsible for that, too, and would have to answer for it. A vague, uneasy feeling crept into the pit of my stomach. I called Aurelia again before I left. When there was no answer, I decided to stop by her house to make sure everything was okay.

After I parked, I sat for a minute in my car to decide the best thing to say, then walked up the crumbling stairs to ring the doorbell.

"Aurelia!" I called out in a cheerful, pleasant voice, then knocked hard when nobody answered. The door pushed open easily as if inviting me inside. Not a good sign. "Aurelia, are you there? It's Dessa Jones." I called again, stepping warily further into the house but with no real sense of danger. "Lacey!" I called out when I got to the stairway, then went halfway up. From where I stood, I could see that a door had been left open. "Lacey, are you up there? It's Dessa Jones. Is your mom here?"

I hesitated before moving farther into the house, then went past the living room with its musty smell and uneven floors, through the messy kitchen, its sink filled with dirty glasses and greasy plates, and finally through the back door into the backyard. A bike stand on the side of the garage was empty. If Lacey had come back home like he said he would, he must have gone back out.

"Aurelia!" I called out again as I headed into the yard.

She was kneeling on the ground. Startled, she looked up, eyes wide and empty as if she didn't know who I was before a tight, uneasy smile crossed her lips.

"I guess you wonder what I'm doing out here, don't you? In the dirt like this. I'm doing some early gardening," she said, then stood up, dropping to the ground the shovel that she'd been holding, dusting dirt off her jeans and blouse. Her face was streaked with sweat, too, mixed with dirt. "Had some junk in here that I needed to uproot. You know how it is with gardens; sometimes you need to make changes when plants crowd things out."

"Hope you don't mind me stopping by. I was on my way to my aunt's place and I wanted to check and make sure everything was okay. Is Lacey here?"

She stooped to the ground and began digging again. "He was here about an hour ago. He must have left. He comes and goes as he pleases these days. I guess that's typical for teenage boys. They come. They go. Half the time they don't tell you where they're going. Is his bike around? He keeps it on that rack over there. If it's gone that means he is. He'll be back when he gets hungry."

"So he was here earlier?"

"Yeah. Why do you ask?" She stood back up to face me.

"Did you have a chance to talk to him?"

"Yeah."

A pile of uprooted plants, shrubs, and flowers lay at her feet, many of them stuffed into two large garbage bags. The well-designed garden once filled with various colors and textures was now shapeless and uncultivated with a gaping hole at the sunny far end of the garden where a large shrub had been.

Aurelia followed my gaze to the empty space. "If you're wondering where Aunt Dahina's plant is, I dug it up."

"Why? It was so beautiful," I said, remembering its wide, glossy leaves.

"It was dying, and that along with all those flax plants reminded me of my late husband. I'll buy flaxseeds at the store from now on if Lacey wants them."

"Did Lacey have a chance to talk to you?" I said, going back to the question I'd asked before.

She brushed off the dirt that clung to her jeans. "You want something to drink?" she asked.

That took me by surprise. "No, it's too early in the day for me."

"Suit yourself." She picked up the shovel and dug up another plant.

"Did he tell you that he was scared of somebody and spent the night on my couch? Did he tell you that?" She was avoiding my questions and I wanted to know why.

"No. But I figured he'd found somewhere to burrow in. Last I heard he was going over to see Tyler Chase, his father's partner. That's what he told me. He didn't mention you one way or the other. Why did he go to your house?"

"He didn't tell you?"

"No."

"But has he been back?" It had become a circular, puzzling conversation.

"I don't see that's any of your business one way or the other," she said, standing up straight again, looking me in the eye.

"Tyler Chase is dead." I waited for a reaction. I wasn't expecting the one I got.

"I heard."

"Did Lacey tell you what he saw?"

"I want you to stay away from my son. You are not his mother, I am, and I will do what is best for him, do you understand me?"

I was taken aback by her tone, riddled as it was with anger. "Of course, I—"

"Let me tell you something else," she said, cutting me off. "He told me what happened, what he saw over there, and I told him to keep what he knows to himself and not to say anything else to anybody, not to you, not the police or anybody else."

"Aurelia, I think you're making a mistake," I said, keeping my tone as neutral and nonjudgmental as I could. "If he told you what he told me, you know that he may have seen things the police need to know about Tyler Chase's death. He told me he was scared, and I really think he needs to talk to them."

"My son has got nothing to be afraid of. I'm here to take care of him. I'll protect him if he needs protection. Do you understand me?" Rage replaced the anger that had been in her voice.

It was the gift that stopped me from saying more, revealing anything that Lacey had told me that maybe he didn't want her to know. My warning came first as a glimmer, as undependable as that can often be. I didn't identify it for a moment and then realized it was the one I'd seen before. The rage seemed to come from nowhere and was the same shade as what had enveloped them both. But it was only her this time, a deep, ugly red of a festering wound. I touched my mother's talisman, held it tight, let it go.

"He's scared and I'm worried about him." I took a chance and told her the truth.

"He'll be fine when everything is over and it soon will be. When things fall into place."

"What is going to fall into place? The money his father left him? That will mean nothing."

Ignoring me, Aurelia turned away and went back to her once beautiful garden. I sat on the bench near the bar where I sat the first time I'd been here, watching her as she ripped things out, tossing dead and living plants onto the growing pile next to her. Maybe this was her way of coping with anger, throwing things away, destroying something she once loved. Maybe it was the only way she could get on with her life.

"Aurelia. Is there anything I can do to help?" I said after watching her for a few minutes. "Anything I can bring you? Any way I can help out with Lacey? I have a friend who's an ex-cop who might be able to give you some advice. Do you want me to call him? You and I were good friends once, and we could be friends again."

I was surprised when she suddenly stopped what she was doing, came over, and sat down beside me. I could see for a moment that young girl who had reached out to a lonely, shy kid and invited her into a popular teenage world. Aurelia Osborne had certainly changed, but there were parts that remained the same. I could see them in her tired eyes and drained face, and in the faint, shy smile she somehow managed. She took off her gardening gloves and held my hand; hers was soft and warm.

"You're a sweet woman, Odessa; you always have been. You were always a nice girl. But you need to stay out of our lives now for your own good as well as for mine. It's important for me and for Lacey that you stay as far away from us as you can get. Lacey will come home soon and things will be fine. It's not your place to worry about him. Do you understand?" Her tone was patient, gentle, nearly the same voice I remembered when I'd been that awkward, lost teenager. I nodded, telling her I understood.

Aurelia went back to digging and tossing, as if she'd forgotten I was still there. I sat a while longer watching her work, then returned to the house, lingering near the stairway for a moment longer than I probably should. I considered calling out to Lacey again, hoping that maybe he'd come home while I was sitting outside with his mother, but then changed my mind.

I went back to my car and drove away, wondering as I did what would become of the two of them. Aurelia was right about wanting me out of their lives, but you can't stop caring about a kid just because somebody tells you to. For the price of warm milk and a safe place to sleep, this sad, frightened boy had trusted me enough to let me enter his world; we'd forged a bond that had to be honored.

Chapter 15

By the time I drove to Aunt Phoenix's place, I'd managed to push Aurelia and Lacey Osborne out of my mind. I didn't know what would happen to them, but I'd been told in no uncertain terms to mind my own business. I had no choice but to do just that. I used my spare key to open my aunt's front door, calling out her name so as not to alarm her, then placed my shopping bags on the kitchen table and the champagne in the refrigerator to keep it cold. When I opened the back door to her small backyard I saw that she was sitting in the sun in one of her backyard chairs, eyes closed, head bobbing, ear buds in ears. She was clearly looking forward to her celebration and had set up an old wobbly card table with a fancy lace tablecloth, matching lace napkins, silverware, and a silver wine bucket for the champagne parked in the middle. I was struck by the care she had put into this celebration and felt another twinge of worry that something troublesome was afoot.

"Aunt Phoenix, I'm here!" I said louder than necessary to overpower whatever music she was listening to. Her music choices and listening volume varied. Some days there was nothing but jazz—Coltrane, Miles Davis, Lee Morgan, the volume turned up. Others were for classical music, always piano, mostly Chopin and Debussy, which she listened to like lullabies. Most days, though, it was singers, those from her past like Billie Holiday, Sarah Vaughan, Ella Fitzgerald, and those just discovered like Beyoncé and Alicia Keys. It was voices this time. When she took out her ear buds, I heard Billie singing "I'll Be Seeing You," a woeful, nostalgic song if ever there was one, which scared the heck out of me.

"Aunt Phoenix, are you okay?"

"Of course I'm okay. About time you got here, I'm hungry," she said gruffly, sounding like her old self; she looked that way, too. She was wearing one of her more festive kaftans, which draped like a tent over her thin body, along with the Birkenstock sandals she'd worn during summers three decades before they became fashionable. It was a far cry from the stylish pantsuit she'd worn when she dropped by my office. I wondered what *that* was about. Her sunbonnet, always present during hot weather, gave her the look of a prematurely aging child. Her copper-colored skin, as flawless as ever, made her look the picture of health. If there was something wrong, it sure wasn't obvious.

"Sorry, I got here as soon as I could," I said with the slightly tightened belly I often felt when encountering my aunt. It was left over from my childhood, when her unconventional manner mystified and occasionally alarmed me. But then she smiled, which always put me at ease.

"Do you need some help?" she asked.

That was a first. "No, I'm fine. It's your birthday; just enjoy yourself."

"Selma Wells said to call her so she can come over for a toast. I think I'll come inside to hurry things along," she added, as if an afterthought.

"Always enjoy your company." I wondered if this would be an opportunity for her moment of truth.

I operate on automatic pilot when I cook, rapidly doing

first things first: quiche in the oven, champagne in the fridge, quickly mixed salad, vinaigrette, tomato "bisque," and croutons, which I'd bought already toasted at the fancy foodie place. My aunt's kitchen was a great place to cook, small but sunny and surprisingly updated. She pulled one of the two chairs that matched the tiny table in the corner of the kitchen close enough to the counter to watch me work. When she wasn't looking, I hastily poured the can of tomato soup into a saucepan, tossing the can back into a shopping bag. I knew I was going too far with the "homemade" business; my aunt probably wouldn't have cared one way or the other. She seemed content just to sit and watch me work, observing every move with the diligence of a culinary student.

"By the way, I'm as healthy as an ox, mule, or any other durable pack animal that comes to mind," she said, her "special" powers once again anticipating the question I was working up enough courage to ask. "And if there was something wrong with me, you'd be the first person I'd tell. I wouldn't have to say anything to Celestine because she'd already know it."

"But I didn't know before," I said, putting down the whisk. I didn't need to mention Darryl's sudden death; she knew what I was talking about and how, despite what I'd been told about the power of the gift, it had given me no warning or hint that he would die. We'd been through this discussion before, and as far as I was concerned it never had an acceptable resolution.

She paused a moment before answering, her voice as patient as she could manage. "As I've told you before, you were so caught up in happiness you didn't listen to what the gift had to say; you didn't want to hear it." I nodded that she was right, but we both knew I'd probably ask her again, and she'd give the same answer. Despite what she said, I didn't understand and never would.

"Maybe I wouldn't hear it if it had something to say about you either," I said, that pang in my heart growing deeper as I picked up the whisk and went back to the vinaigrette.

"Because I'll know when I'm on my way out and I'll tell you myself. And that's why you have that silver ribbon of hair running down the side of your face," she said, her voice a bit sharper as she took our conversation in a direction I hadn't seen but should have known was coming.

"I was going to bring that up." I checked the quiche and added cream and other ingredients to the tomato soup.

"Be grateful!"

"Huh? Be grateful?"

She chuckled, which she didn't do often. "It's a reminder, Odessa, like you tie a ribbon around your finger. It's saying you can't take life for granted, that it can change in a beat, that it's unpredictable, so you have no idea what will happen next, and that's the beauty of it. You've got the gift to warn and the streak to remind you to take every day as a blessing. They put a check on each other."

I was both annoyed and confused. "Then what good is either one? I go to bed with black hair and wake up with a streak of gray. What kind of message is that?"

"Just that life is more twisted than simple, too quick and mysterious to know, like that streak of dazzling blue sky that shows up on a rainy day or that dark, hovering cloud that peeks out when the sun is bright."

"I suppose that's one way of looking at it," I muttered, taking the quiche out of the oven to let it cool.

"If you're that worried about that hair, dye it again. Something interesting."

"I'm thinking pink."

"I wouldn't go that far. But do understand it will come back."

I groaned and put the finishing touches on the tomato "bisque," which included fresh chopped basil.

After offering this wisdom, the guest of honor returned to the backyard and sat down at the table. I brought out sparkling water, the champagne, and three flutes, for the two of us and Selma Wells whenever she came. The tomato "bisque" had thickened enough to live up to its name, and the toasted croutons and chopped basil added the colorful lift I was hoping for. I served the soup in her blue cobalt bowls, which gave our first course an elegant flair. The quiche had cooled by then, and I brought it outside on a serving platter along with the salad and our plates. I chastised myself again as I sliced it for not coming up with a worthier brunch. Also remembering with a touch of discomfort that despite its convenience, this dish had a checkered history. It had been the centerpiece of my strange afternoon with Aurelia, and a presence at the ill-fated Osborne brunch. What I had always considered my go-to-in-a-pinch quiche, as dependable as my go-to pound cake, was in need of a gastronomic vacation. But the quiche was still tasty, and if my aunt knew of or guessed its past, it didn't seem to faze her. Although she didn't care for eggs, she liked cheese and loved collards, and this had both.

"Well, Dessa, you've outdone yourself this time," she said, as I cut her a second slice. I breathed a sigh of relief. "The homemade soup was good, too. I hope it wasn't too much trouble to prepare," she said with just enough emphasis on "homemade" and a quick eyebrow lift to tell me she knew its true origin.

"No trouble at all," I said lightly, playing along. As I took the leftovers back into the kitchen, the doorbell rang on cue.

Selma Wells and my aunt had lived next door to each other for as long as I could remember. Through the years they had become what my aunt called "some-timey" friends, which meant they went through short periods where they got on each other's nerves but because they were neighbors always found their way back.

Like many black women of a certain age, there was nary a line on Selma's smooth skin, which was the color of light brown sugar, save the smattering of mahogany freckles lightly sprinkled on her forehead and cheeks. Although they were roughly the same age, give a decade or so, the two women were totally different. Where my aunt was thin and wiry, Selma was plump and soft. Aunt Phoenix had been married once, then separated. I wasn't sure what had happened to the relationship and had no intention of asking. I also suspected she'd had more than her share of lovers; I didn't ask about that either. I did know that she was proud of her single status and was never shy about sharing her thoughts on marriage. Selma, on the other hand, had been married to her husband, Alfred, for forty-odd years but never ceased complaining about him—usually to my aunt, much to her annoyance. *Why the heck doesn't she just divorce the fool?* she had told me more than once. But Aunt Phoenix could be a good listener, and it formed the basis of their tenuous relationship.

Another big difference was that Aunt Phoenix preferred her own company and made no secret of the fact. She was a joyful loner and loved the solitude of her yard, sunlight on her back, ear buds in her ears, book in her hands. Selma, on the other hand, was a ceaseless party giver, and her yard, separated from my aunt's by a rickety fence, was always filled with activity. Lately, she'd been babysitting twin boys, both mischievous and exceptionally noisy. My aunt liked children, but at a safe distance, and those two kids were too close for comfort. I suspected that they had been the source of her and Selma's misunderstanding, which had apparently been healed by the plant Selma had recently given her.

"Nice to see you again, Odessa," said Selma, holding a bouquet of grocery store roses in her hand, a gift I assumed for my aunt. "Did Phoenix tell you I was coming to toast her on her birthday?"

"Yes, she did. Do you know which one it is?" I asked in a low voice.

"Whatever it is, she's much older than me," Selma said, with a wink; I wasn't sure if I should take her at her word. She followed me into the kitchen, glancing longingly at what was left of the quiche on the counter.

"Would you like me to cut you a slice?"

"That would be nice. I'll take it home with me. Please put these in water for the birthday girl so they won't wilt," she said, handing me the bouquet.

"I'm sure she'll love them." That was a boldfaced lie. Aunt Phoenix always complained that the fragrance had been bred out of roses, so they were the one flower she couldn't abide. "She's in the backyard." I hoped Selma kept the birthday girl crack to herself.

I didn't have to worry. After finding a vase for the flowers and packing away the leftovers, I went outside to find the two women chatting amiably and impatiently holding their champagne as they waited for me.

As I lifted mine for a toast, I tried to think of something profound to say, then ended up speaking from my heart. "To my aunt Phoenix, whose name suits her well!"

We sipped our champagne and Selma held her glass out for more. "Just what is a phoenix? I've always heard about them but never knew exactly what they were."

"A firebird that rises from its own ashes," my aunt said with a cackle. "This old bird will drink to that."

The two women took generous gulps in agreement.

"Does everyone in your family have an odd name?" Selma asked.

"I guess you might say that, but I've never thought of it

that way. Rosemary, Odessa's mother's name, is an herb of remembrance and fidelity. Celestine, the name of my younger sister, means 'heavenly'—although she's anything but—and of course there's me. Fire. I don't know what my parents had in mind, but it does come down to the elements of earth, sky, and fire."

"How interesting!" said Selma.

"Is that really why they did it?" This was the first I'd heard of this theory. I wondered if Phoenix had made it up for the occasion and was just pulling Selma's leg, as she was known to do.

My aunt shrugged. "Maybe they just liked the way the names sounded," she said, which was probably closer to the truth.

Selma gave a slight smile, as if she wasn't completely sure about what she'd just heard but was willing to suspend disbelief in honor of her friend's birthday. "Well, I don't know about you rising from your own ashes, Phoenix, but you've done wonders with that plant I gave you. Thanks again for taking it."

"No problem, I just hope it's worth the trouble."

We shifted our attention from the champagne to the large plant that now occupied more than its share of space in a sunny patch at the outer edge of my aunt's garden. Both women, obviously pleased with themselves, headed toward it. From where I sat, I could tell that its tropical appearance was strangely out of place in my aunt's vegetable and flower garden. The leaves were veined and bright green, a plant that clearly needed sun. I put down my champagne and went over to where they were standing.

I stopped in my tracks when I got there. With a start, I remembered my aunt's words about the plant earning its own keep and about it being worth the trouble. What kind of plant was this? It looked vaguely familiar. I examined it closely, then gasped. Marijuana had just been made legal in Jersey. Had these two mistakenly—or otherwise—planted marijuana?

"It seems to be doing very well; you never know how a transplant like this will grow," Selma said.

"I just hope it works. I'm sick and tired of spending money that could be better used on other things," said my aunt.

I had to say something, and I had to say it quick. "Aunt Phoenix! You can't grow something like this! For one thing, it may be legal, but you need a license to do it. You just can't plant weed out of the blue. Not only that, but it's—"

The expressions of both women stopped me mid-sentence. Aunt Phoenix spoke up first. "Odessa, have you lost your mind? What the heck are you talking about? What do you think this plant is? Don't tell me you think it's marijuana!"

My stomach tightened. "Well . . . I . . ."

Selma seemed to lose her breath. When she regained it, along with her composure, she glared at me in disgust. "Do you think I would give your aunt an illegal drug to grow?"

"Actually, I think it's considered more herb than drug, and I don't think it's illegal anymore, especially if it's for medicinal—"

"Shush! Best be quiet and sit down and listen!" Aunt Phoenix said, but what I heard was: *Close your mouth before I close it for you.* It was a voice I hadn't heard since I was six. Without another word, I returned with them to the table and sat down, head hung low like a scolded child. "That plant is not marijuana. It's a castor bean plant. You use its seeds to kill moles, those nasty little creatures who burrow in and out of my garden like it belongs to them. You put the seeds in their little molehill and eventually they die. Unpleasant as it sounds, I've heard it works."

Still angry, Selma took over where my aunt left off. "Your aunt was kind enough to replant it in her garden when I started watching those twins after school. Castor bean seeds look like nuts and that appeals to kids. If one of my little imps took it into his head to bite into one, chew it, and swallow it, it would kill him. I'd end up in jail for manslaughter, which is why you don't plant it around kids."

"Ricin. Castor bean seeds contain ricin, one of the deadliest poisons in the world. I don't have any kids around here, save one who likes to think she's grown," Aunt Phoenix continued, throwing me a withering glance. "If I wanted to plant weed, Odessa, I certainly wouldn't grow it in my backyard where everybody could see it. What kind of a fool do you take me for? If I need an altered sense of reality, I'll take a sip of cherry brandy!"

Selma, slightly surprised, gave Phoenix a critical glance at the mention of cherry brandy, then took what looked like a cleansing gulp of champagne.

A quick apology was needed. "I'm so sorry. Please forgive me, both of you. I should have known better!"

"Yes, you should have," said Aunt Phoenix.

"But it's such a beautiful plant and it looks so familiar with those leaves and everything, and you always see pictures of marijuana, so I thought—"

"Whatever you thought was wrong, and I certainly have no idea how marijuana looks," Selma said, cutting me off, self-righteous to the end. Aunt Phoenix rolled her eyes.

Humiliated, I went to take another look at the plant to determine where I'd seen it and how I could have made such a mistake. Then I remembered. It had been in Aurelia Osborne's backyard, Aunt Dahina's gift, she had told me, dug up this morning by the roots and piled on top of the other "dead" plants she was clearing out of her garden. But its leaves were bright green and as alive as this one.

When I returned to the table, Selma was complaining about her husband. Unaccustomed as she was to afternoon drinking, the champagne had made her louder than usual. Even though she was nodding attentively, my aunt had discreetly turned off her hearing aid, the unmistakable sign that she didn't want to hear what you had to say.

"Let me help you clear these things up," she said to me, and quickly began gathering up our dishes. I smiled to myself; I knew my aunt well.

"Thanks, that would be great."

"Thank you," she whispered as we headed into the kitchen.

Selma continued her rant, apparently unaware that my aunt had disappeared. "Well, I guess that's my hint that it's time to go," I heard her say to herself when she realized she was alone before she joined us in the kitchen.

"I'm so sorry, Selma, alcohol in the middle of the day makes me sleepy . . . and rude," my aunt said, offering an apology.

I guess cherry brandy doesn't count, I said to myself.

But they hugged like old friends before Selma left carrying the remains of the collard green quiche. After she was gone, my aunt took up her seat near the kitchen table, and watched me as I washed and dried the dishes.

"Odessa, you have something on your mind you can't shake," she said as I put away her blue cobalt soup bowls. "I hope that mess about that plant isn't still bothering you. It's funny now that I think about it." She chuckled, for the second time this day. A rare sound and one I loved to hear.

"No, it's not that. Do you remember that text you sent me a while ago, about bitterness being like a cancer that feeds upon its host? How come you sent it when you did?"

My aunt shrugged. "Sometimes things just come to me and I pass them on to you, and that was one of those times. A gift thing. Does it mean something important?'

"I don't know yet," I said, as I dried the last dish and put it back in my aunt's neat pantry. Aurelia Osborne had been digging up that castor bean plant as fast as she could. What was her rush? Lacey was a teenager and so cautious about nuts, deathly allergic, as he'd told me twice, that he'd never touch them. His note said he was going home, yet he must have left soon after getting there. Was he running from something? What was he afraid of? With every hint the gift bestows, I knew that the boy was in danger. I had to find out why.

Chapter 16

I had no idea where I should go, what I should do, how I should feel. My first impulse was to call the police, always your initial thought when somebody needs protecting. But my recent interactions with the local cops had been bumpy at best. Up until a few weeks ago, I was considered a material witness, not the best recommendation for them listening to me. Besides, when I contacted them I had to have a sound reason, one based on concrete fact, not suspicion or speculation. What would I say, that I was worried about a boy I barely knew who might have disappeared, though his mother claimed he wasn't missing, who may have witnessed a murder not yet declared a murder? That sounded crazy even to me. Mentioning the gift and my foreboding sense of danger was out of the question. Every fear I had was based upon speculation. Was my imagination working overtime?

Before doing anything, I had to stop by Aurelia's house again, if for no other reason than to see if Lacey had returned. Until I knew otherwise, I should not listen to the gift's foreboding. Aurelia hinted this morning that her son came and went at will, like teenagers are known to do. There was a chance he'd come home again after I left for my aunt's house and was doing nothing more dangerous now than talking to friends while playing video games in his room. Aurelia had identified the plant she threw out as a gift from her aunt Dahina, but she may not have known the seeds were poisonous. She claimed the plant was dying, and for all I knew it may have been. I was nobody's gardener by anyone's imagination; I could hardly manage a bed of impatiens. There had been a pile of plants and flowers, including flax and petunias, which she said reminded her of her dead husband. Aurelia wanted to restart her life, and I could appreciate that. She deserved that chance.

As I pulled up to Aurelia's home, my suspicious notions had turned into second thoughts. I was grateful I'd kept them to myself and not told anyone, especially the police; the thought of that made me cringe. The wise thing for me to do was simply turn my car around and head back home like I had good sense. I glanced in her driveway as I drove past her house. Her car was parked there, a good sign, but the rack that held Lacey's bike was empty. She was home, but he wasn't. What did that mean? Probably nothing.

I drove around the block again, not yet able to shake the nagging feeling that something wasn't right. I considered talking to Aurelia again, and tried to come up with some good reason to be stopping by. She'd made it clear this morning that my concerns about her and her child were intrusive and unwelcomed. If I showed up again asking questions, it could be within her rights to get some kind of restraining order against me. I suspected the local police would have little problem granting it. I drove around the block a third time, hoping to see Lacey rounding the corner, pulling into his driveway, letting me know he was safe where he was supposed to be.

Yet I couldn't get the memory of that trembling boy out of my mind.

Who do you think is going to kill you? I'd asked.

I don't want to say, he'd told me.

That had struck me as strange when he'd said it, and stranger still how quickly he changed to a different subject, that he was thirsty. He may have been, but then he changed again to his father and the relationship they had. He'd never answered my question, just avoided it altogether.

I don't want to say. I don't want to say.

A thought came to me that slammed straight down to my gut.

What if it was Aurelia? What if he couldn't bring himself to tell me that the person who wanted to kill him was his mother?

I tried to dismiss it. Aurelia clearly loved her son; I was sure of that. Yet even parents who love their children often do them harm, without realizing they've done it. I recalled that day in her garden, the brief time I'd spent with the two of them, and how she mocked him, dismissing the memory of his father, playfully trying to force-feed him that quiche like he was a little kid. It was insulting and demeaning, especially for a teenage boy struggling to find his place after his father's death, trying to become a man. Violence wasn't always a physical stroke; words could be every bit as lethal. Her words and actions had been poisonous. Sitting with her this morning, I'd been reminded of when I'd known her as a girl. She was my friend when nobody else was. I knew there was a part of me that simply didn't want to believe that she would harm her son.

And then there was the gift. It was occasionally undependable, but often it was spot-on; it wouldn't let my fears about Lacey go. Aurelia said her son had come and gone, but where had he gone? I recalled his words to Erika when she teased him about being afraid of Juniper. She'd asked where he went when he got scared. Mostly the park, he said, because he and his father rode their bikes there and it felt good to see things they'd seen together. What harm would it do to take a look? Nobody had to know.

I headed to the county park that I knew so well, the one where I once walked and jogged with Darryl, where we'd sit on the benches near the cycling paths taking in its beauty. It was where I went when I was sick of being home by myself and needed another place to cry. I'd gone there the day of Charlie Risko's murder, and it had offered me an escape from what was then a terrible office situation, given me peace when I needed it most. It made sense that Lacey might come here, too.

Each season brought rewards: golden and red leaves in the fall, kids sledding in the snow in winter, spring itself, a reminder of renewal. This was summer, the season of roses, and the rose garden, planted and maintained by dedicated park volunteers, was the pride of the park and the towns that surrounded it, wealthy and struggling alike. Even strangers knew better than to pick the flowers. If you sat there long enough, you could catch the elusive fragrance of roses, despite Aunt Phoenix's claim that they no longer had a scent. I sat on one of the benches near the garden, a place I knew well, closed my eyes for a while, listening to park noises: children laughing in the distance, dogs barking, people walking by. I wondered if Lacey and Osborne had ridden on the nearby bicycle path. If Lacey had, sooner or later he would pass by; there was no other place to go. It was late afternoon, still day, but the park closed at dusk. I stayed a while longer, waiting and hoping, but the last of the riders pedaled by and Lacey wasn't among them.

Had he gone back to my house? He said he felt safe there. I drove back home, hoping to see his bike lying in my driveway or find him sitting on the front stairs patiently waiting. He wasn't here either. I drove around town a while longer, up and down streets I barely knew, keeping an eye out for his bike parked near a 7-Eleven or Burger King, looking out for a kid riding fast down the street trying to make himself invisible.

Dusk passed quickly and evening was setting in. I suspected the truth was that Lacey didn't want to be found. Maybe he'd gone back home, after all, and my suspicions were foolish, but what if they weren't? I needed to talk things over with someone who could offer insight with no judgment attached. Lennox Royal came to mind. This once-upon-a-time cop with cop's instincts was one of the few people I knew I could share my thoughts with, no matter how odd they might seem, who would offer a sympathetic ear and a professional opinion. He was good company, had good advice, and a good plate of barbecued chicken, if everything I was thinking meant nothing.

Lennox might also have insight into a kid like Lacey who loved swords and chess. He'd said the game had been special to him because his grandfather had taught him, just like Casey Osborne had taught his son. Besides that, I could almost taste Royal's tangy barbecue sauce on my tongue. I pulled into a parking spot just down from the restaurant ready for some chicken and began thinking about my sides.

Then in the next moment I knew where Lacey had gone. It was to that last place he had been with his father, that last game they were to play the day he died. Just as quickly, the boy's question came back to me again.

Who do you think is going to kill you?

I don't want to say.

What if it wasn't Aurelia but Mona Osborne? He knew someone had been there before Tyler Chase died, and that it had been a woman. What if he guessed it was Mona? She might have known Lacey had come to see Tyler, who would have mentioned it when he rejoined her in bed or wherever they were. Mona likely knew about Lacey's history of setting fires, too. He could easily be blamed for setting the one that had burned Chase's town house. Lacey suspected Mona had something to do with his father's death, before the police determined that Osborne had died of natural causes. What if Lacey was right? Mona must know that the police might take another look at her if Red was off the hook—natural causes or not. Tyler Chase probably knew more than he was saying.

Look what you've brought down on us. After everything we've been through, everything we planned, and it ends up here with her. Everything I've done for us!

Those were Mona's words to Tyler the night of Tanya's disastrous dinner. I knew there was more to that relationship than was commonly known. Maybe Lacey had guessed that, too.

If Lacey confronted Mona in her home, there were half a dozen ways the scene could play out: Mona could shoot him as an intruder or claim she heard somebody break into the house, panicked, and ran downstairs to confront him. She was pregnant and vulnerable and newly widowed. The kid was "troubled" and she was frightened. She could claim he threatened her. He was a big kid, big enough for somebody to think she was telling the truth, particularly if she claimed that she knew he'd killed Tyler Chase and set that fire. Mona Osborne could do or say anything she wanted to and she would be believed.

I drove fast to the Osborne estate, my thoughts racing ahead of me, fearful of what I would find. When I drove up, I knew immediately that Lacey was here and he'd been in a hurry. His bike had been left in the driveway leading to the back door, tossed aside as it had been at my place, just waiting for someone to drive over it.

The back door to the kitchen was open and I stepped inside. Everything that had happened the last time I was here came back in a terrible flash, except nothing was soiled, everything was sparkling and clean again; from the stainless-steel appliances to the white granite counters, it was as if nobody had died here and nothing bad had happened. The lights were twinkling in the ceiling, so I knew someone was here or had come and left.

Where would I find him? I stepped inside cautiously, took a deep breath, both to calm myself and to detect any hint of that dreadful forewarning scent I never wanted to smell. There was nothing, thank God. Lacey was still alive if he was here. Mona must not be at home.

"Lacey. I know you're here." I walked farther into the kitchen toward the closed door that led to Osborne's study. It was the place where Lacey had to be. I knocked softly.

"Lacey?" I opened the door and peeked inside.

He sat at the table in front of the chessboard, as if preparing to play. I watched him for a while, wondering what I should say, the best way to find out how he was feeling, what was going on. When he looked up, I could see he'd been crying. I expected as much. He had found his way back to the game and this room, which held memories he wasn't ready to let go; I wasn't ready to make him let them go. I sat across the table where his father once sat and watched him, saying nothing until he was ready to talk. I knew we'd have to leave soon, before Mona returned from wherever she'd gone. I'm sure he knew it, too. When he finally looked at me, his eyes were swollen and red.

"I killed him," he said. "I'm the one who killed him!"

I drew back, his words hitting me so hard I could think of nothing to say, couldn't breathe for a second. He seemed so certain, so sure of it, I wondered for a moment if he could be telling the truth, even though I didn't think it could be possible. He continued as if determined to convince me.

"I killed him because I was the one who gave him the stuff she made, that flax junk she made for his smoothies. Don't you remember? I told you about that! You need to remember!"

I tried to recall what he'd said last night but hadn't paid close attention to every word. I told him what I could. "You said you gave your dad stuff for his smoothie the day before he died. I don't understand why you think that killed him."

He slammed his hand on the table, impatiently knocking the chess pieces off the board and onto the floor. "Because she knew. She knew!"

I picked the pieces up, carefully placing them back on the squares where I thought they had been.

"You're talking about your mother, aren't you? What do you think she knew?" I said, knowing what I suspected to be the truth, but I had to hear it from him.

"That the seeds were poison."

"What seeds are you talking about?" I wanted to make sure that he understood what he was accusing her of.

He looked at me, his eyes incredulous. "The seeds from the plant she was getting rid of." He paused, making sure I was the one who understood. "You know when I left your house and went home? When I got there she was digging up that plant she was always watering, said she was throwing it away. I asked her why and she didn't tell me, but I knew why. When I was little my aunt Dahina used to smack my hands whenever I picked up one of those seeds from that plant. She'd smack them so hard that my dad yelled at her for doing it. She told me later never to touch those seeds because if I ate one it would kill me. Just like nuts. Faster than nuts."

"And your mom knew that, too?"

"I never went near it. I would get flaxseeds and grind them up for smoothies for me and my dad to drink, and that was okay because I did it all the time. But that day was different. She told me that she'd put nuts in it by mistake. She said it was okay except for the nuts and left it on the counter. She knew I would take it to him and I did. So I killed him." He fell back in his chair like the air had been knocked out of him. "It's still there, if you don't believe me. Go in the kitchen and look. That's where my dad kept it, in a fancy jar near his blender. He must have had it the day he died. I killed him," he repeated, sounding more sure of himself than before. "Go! Go and look!"

I went into the kitchen like Lacey told me. The glass jar was still there, but half filled now. He was right. I thought about that morning again, Osborne coming in, acting nasty, demanding more salt in the food. But he was holding another drink that day, one in a shot glass that could have been anything. He had it in his hand when he came into the kitchen before he mixed himself his health drink. I remembered his fancy blender, admiring it at the time, and noticed how fresh those strawberries and blueberries he put into it were. He'd opened the container with the seeds, but he hadn't added them. I remembered that, too. He smelled it, wrinkled up his nose like a finicky kid sniffing something gross, and screwed the top right back, twisting it tight. Louella and I had chuckled about him and his "healthy" drink. It was the last time either of us had laughed that day. I didn't know what killed Casey Osborne, maybe his bad health, natural causes, like the medical examiner had said, but I knew it wasn't from drinking a smoothie made with castor bean seeds that Lacey had given him. I just had to convince his son. When I went back into the office, he was carefully studying the board, putting the chess pieces back where he remembered them being.

"Lacey, I was here in the kitchen when your father mixed his smoothie. He came in while I was cooking. I watched him as he added fruit and almond milk to his blender, but he didn't add anything from that jar. That was all, just the fruit. He didn't touch whatever you brought him. I know that for a fact."

Lacey stared at me a long time without speaking, as if his

eyes could pull any truth out of me that I was trying to hide. When he spoke his voice was so low I could barely hear him.

"Do you promise?"

"I promise."

"Do you swear it, swear it on . . . on your, your husband's honor?"

That took me aback, but I knew Darryl wouldn't mind and had more honor than he'd ever need.

"I swear it on my husband's honor."

Lacey's breath left him, as if he'd been holding it in, which he must have been. He nodded as if accepting it, studied the board a little longer, then looked at me like he'd just remembered something. "Then how come so much was gone?"

The question went through me, leaving me without breath. I didn't want to tell him what I feared until I knew for sure.

"When did you get here?"

"About an hour ago. I rode in the park, then up and down the street. I thought about my dad and what my mom did and how mad I was at her, and that maybe she'd try to kill me like she killed him."

"Do you really believe that?"

"I don't know."

"Then you came here?"

"I wanted to throw the seed stuff away before people found out that my mom did it. I started thinking about Mona, too, that maybe she might put it in her drinks and that it might hurt the baby. I used my key to get in. Then I started thinking about my dad, and how he might have drunk it, and I just came in here and didn't want to move. Then you came."

"Mona wasn't here when you came?"

"No. I called her, but she didn't answer. I figured she must have gone out. I was mad at Mona because I thought maybe she'd killed my dad, but now I know it wasn't her. I thought it was me, but that's not true either, right?"

"Right, it was natural causes," I said again, although I wasn't absolutely sure about that either.

"You know what," he said, a smile that wasn't quite one crossing his lips. "I thought about what you said, about having a little brother or sister and how it would be part of my dad. I knew I had to warn Mona, too, and that was another reason I came."

"To warn Mona before it was too late?"

"Yeah."

"Stay here for a few minutes. I want to check upstairs and see if maybe she's up there, maybe taking a nap or just not coming downstairs. Don't move, okay?"

"Do you want me to come with you?" He sensed something was wrong.

"No, stay here. I just want to check upstairs to see if she's there. If she's not we're going to leave when I come back, understand?"

He shook his head that he did. I closed the door tight behind me when I left.

I'd forgotten how spacious and luxurious this house was with its abstract paintings that belonged in a museum, sculptures, and massive fireplace, which I hadn't noticed before because of the crowd milling around, the antique rugs and long, stylish couches, with space enough to seat fifty people comfortably. A sense of dread filled me as I approached the staircase. Mona Osborne had floated down it that day, elegant and graceful in her pretty little dress with her pretty little smile. The sun had poured in through these huge picture windows as if blessing every move she made. It was dark now, the night replacing the sun. I took the stairs, step by step, until it stopped me: the overwhelming stink of nutmeg.

Chapter 17

I ran downstairs, tripping over my feet on the way back down. Voices were coming from the kitchen. It was Aurelia talking to her son. I touched my mother's talisman, its hard, smooth surface reminding me of her strength and my own. I moved through the living room, dreading each step, past the kitchen, toward that tiny office. I had to make her face what she had done.

I approached the small, close room as quietly as I could, and stood just outside the door cautiously watching. I knew what I had to do but was unwilling to break into the conversation until they were ready to end it. Aurelia sat next to Lacey, still in her dirty jeans, her face soiled with dust as I'd seen her earlier this morning; she had come straight here. She'd pulled the chair that I'd been sitting in, where his father had once sat, next to him, near enough to touch him, but not quite. Lacey had moved, shifting as far away as he could, as if fearful she would hurt him. But she was his mother, and there was no way he could get away from that. After a while, she stopped talking. She had said everything she wanted to, but he hadn't had his say. Looking her in the face, his eyes filled with anger, he demanded to know the truth.

"Tell me why you tried to kill him."

She shifted away from him as if puzzled by his question.

"How do you know that?"

"Because of the seeds you put into that stuff you gave me to give him. The ones from Aunt Dahina's plant."

"There was nothing in that but flax. You know that, Lacey. I told you that. And walnuts because I made a mistake. An honest mistake. That's all. Nothing more. It was just flax and—"

"Shut up, you liar!" I didn't think such fury could be held in so few words.

She dropped her head, nodding, as if accepting that he knew the truth and there was no use lying anymore. She spoke loudly when she answered him, as if volume alone would sear her words into his heart and make them acceptable. It was the way a desperate mother might yell at an angry child: *Listen to me, believe me, because I tell you it is true.*

"I wanted everything he had to go to you, don't you understand that? I did it for you." The glimmer was back, reddish purple again, and brought to mind the raging color that had shadowed them both on her porch that first day. Her bitterness, like the cancer that it was, fed only upon her now, letting her son go free.

"Why?" Lacey screamed out the word, ignoring her answer, his voice as shrill as hers had been. "Why?" he said again, softer this time, and she moved away from him, shaking her head as if she didn't understand the question.

"I told you why," she said impatiently, her tone sharper, that of a mother not wanting her word disputed.

"I was next, right? Like you tried to kill my dad. Sooner or later you'd put poison in something for me to drink, just like you did for him."

Aurelia fell back against the chair as if her son had struck her, head dropping to her chest. When she looked at him again, her eyes were filled with the same anguish that had been in her voice.

"How could you think I would kill you, Lace?" she said, calling him a pet name that was probably just between the two of them.

"That's what your love brings," he said, his tone as reasonable as an old man calling the truth as he saw it, but then he turned into a child again, his voice a whine. "And don't call me that again. Ever! And what about Mona? Were you going to kill her and the baby, too?"

It was time for me to enter and step into their conversation. Lacey didn't know yet that Mona was dead, but now was not the moment to tell him. He would only blame himself for that, too, spiraling into that darkness that held him when he took refuge in this room. Events that had nothing to do with him had to play themselves out first.

"Aurelia," I said, and they both looked up.

She was startled, her eyes wide with surprise that turned to annoyance. "I told you to leave us alone. What are you doing here?"

"I asked her to come," said Lacey, in the voice of a kid again, but one far younger than he was. He was right, I realized, because he had asked me, by way of the gift and the bond we had without knowing we had it.

Aurelia took a breath, let it out slow as if calming herself down, waiting to get it back before she said anything, even though we both knew there was nothing she could say.

"We need to talk now, Aurelia, but let's go somewhere else," I said, pushing aside my feelings toward her and finding the voice of the teenage girl who had once been her friend. She nodded as if she understood, her face empty and haunted. Lacey didn't need to know what she was going to say, but I had to hear it, for myself. I led her from the kitchen into that vast living room where everything had begun. We sat down on one of the long, luxurious couches near the staircase, sinking into its plush cushioned depths. I could smell nutmeg floating down from upstairs.

"Mona Osborne is dead," I said.

"So it finally worked." Her thin, cruel smile unnerved me, and I touched my mother's talisman again, its smooth, hard surface reassuring me as only it could. Yet it wasn't for protection this time but wisdom to give me the words to say to this woman, who had been an older sister during a vulnerable time, whom I had once loved. I thought back to something that Lennox Royal had told me once. He was as much an expert on evil and its ways as Aunt Phoenix on impossibilities unseen and unheard. Everyone had a devil living somewhere inside him, he'd said, and all that it took for it to be wakened was a poke, which had made me wonder about my own slumbering demon and what it would take to wake it up. I hoped I never found out.

"Why did you do it?"

"Why do you think?" she said. "It's like I just told my son. I wanted to make sure Lacey got the money. I wanted to make sure that he was taken care of. I did it for my son. Who knows what Mona would have done if all his money had come to her and that baby she was carrying."

I turned away from her in disgust. She lightly touched my face, trying to bring my attention back to her. A chill crept through my body, turning my stomach so hard I thought I might be sick. I faced her eye to eye, because I was sick of the lie she was telling, and swiped her hand off my face.

"You didn't do it for him; you did it for yourself. You tried to kill the boy's father even though you know how they loved each other, and how much it would hurt him."

She shrugged casually, as if she didn't give a damn one way or the other, but I could see that it was forced. "I got tired of the stuff Casey put me through; leaving me like he did for her was the final thing. I knew sooner or later it would get one of them, like a seed you plant that finally comes to bloom. You want to know how I did it, don't you?" she said, cocking her head to one side, as if sharing a secret like she used to do when we were girls sitting in the back of her aunt's old car, pretending she was our chauffeur and we were rich and famous, laughing and cutting up. I pulled away, and she grabbed my hand again like she had in her garden this morning, holding it so tightly it was hard to snatch away.

"I knew he drank that stuff, trying to be healthy for this woman like he never did for me, old as he was, sick as he was. I didn't know which of them would use it first and how long it would take. But sooner or later one or both of them would be dead. I'd just bide my time until it happened, like I told him that day at his party, I'd have the last laugh, and I did."

I remembered her words. I'd taken them for the rant of a bitter, drunk woman, but she meant what she said. She was right; she'd had it.

"The thing about castor bean seeds is you got to grind them up good for them to work," she added as if I'd asked her, matter-of-fact, as if I needed the information. "Even if you're killing moles, like Aunt Dahina used to do. You crush them first. I had my own moles to kill. I had to do it with gloves because touching them when they're ground can be chancy. I ground it like I was grinding up flax, little by little, saving it bit by bit. I threw the blender away so Lacey wouldn't use it again. I thought it would take ten hours to kill him; that's what I heard. But maybe I was wrong. He went fast."

"You didn't kill him. He died of natural causes," I said, throwing the truth in her face as if it would make a difference.

She continued as if she hadn't heard me. "After he died, every time I came by to visit, I wished her dead. I added a tiny bit each time, little by little, to the jar where I saw they kept their seeds. I knew she would use them, taking care of herself like she did, and they got her, too, didn't they?"

I felt sick again and so disgusted I looked at the floor, then the ceiling and the velvet couch, anywhere but at her.

"Do you understand why I did it?"

"What is going to happen to your son?" I asked.

Lacey walked into the room before she could answer my question. I realized he must have been standing at the door listening to us for all this time. He glared at her, then at me, unsure of what to say next or maybe how he felt. She beckoned him to come and sit by her on the couch, which was wide enough for far more than the three of us. It was as if she thought he was a little boy again, who might want to cozy up to his mother. He stood far away from both of us, scowling down at her as if she were the child and he the adult.

"I loved my dad. More than I ever loved you. I hate you now," he said.

She reached to touch his hand, but he snatched it away. "Come and sit down here with me for a minute. Don't say that, because you don't mean it."

He violently shook his head, as if to show her just how much he disagreed. He was telling the truth as he knew it. He might not feel that way next month, or a year or even five years later, but now he did, and we both knew it.

"You killed Mona. That's why the jar is half-full. You would have killed me, too, because that's what you do. That's what your love brings," he said, repeating what he'd said to her in the kitchen.

He turned away from both of us, going back to where he'd been in the study that had been his haven. I sat a while longer as I gathered my thoughts about how best to comfort him and make the call I had to make. I left her sitting on the couch; she had nowhere else to go.

* * *

Lacey was sitting where he was before when I came into the room, holding the black knight in his hand like I hold my talisman for luck, protection, and memories.

"Is my mom going to jail?" he asked when I sat down across from him.

"I don't know," I said, although I was sure she probably was.

When he looked up at me, his eyes demanded that I tell him the truth, all but saying, *Don't BS me, because I can't take any more of that.* "If people are found guilty of a crime that's usually where they end up," I finally said.

He sighed an old man's sigh. "Maybe she didn't mean to do it. Maybe she's sorry. Do you think maybe she's sorry now?"

"I hope she is."

We sat there a while longer, me putting off what I needed to do because I had to tell him first. Finally, I just said it. "Mona is dead, and I have to call the police and tell them what your mom told me."

He nodded that he understood. "I'm going to see my mom first, okay?"

"Yeah, she'd like that." I didn't know what he was going to say to her, but it was none of my business. This would be the last time they would have this chance. I was sure of that. While he was gone, I made the call I needed to make.

Apparently, Sundays were still on Detective Ramos's beat. He was the same officer who had answered the call three weeks ago and found Casey Osborne dead on the kitchen floor. He looked grayer and plumper and still had the woebegone look of a man who would rather be home watching ESPN on a Sunday afternoon. He immediately recognized the kitchen but not me. I'm not sure what that said about either of us.

"Tried the front door, and when nobody answered I remembered this back door, so thought I'd try it," he said when he stepped inside. "Sorry about that. It's a big house. You're the one who called about the dead body upstairs, right? Accidental, I assumed. And you are, uh, the housekeeper, cook? Weren't you here before when I came? Do you live here?" He gazed around the spotless kitchen, remarkably cleaner than what it had been on his first visit.

"I'm Dessa Jones, the caterer who—"

"Oh God, now I remember," he said, with a scowl that made me wish he hadn't. "The lady with the dicey jelly? You still cooking for these people?"

Momentarily stunned, it took a moment for me to gather my wits enough to explain what had happened. For Aunt Phoenix's sake, I also added that the "jelly" was fine.

He settled down on a counter stool, and gazed around the room. "That's the door to that office study, right? It's all coming back now. I'm going to go over again what you just told me, to see if I got it all, okay? You are telling me that the owner of this house, Mona Osborne, a pregnant lady and the widow of the man who died in this kitchen, is dead upstairs and the woman responsible, his ex-wife, is sitting on the living room couch. Is that what you just told me?"

I nodded that he was right, realizing as the words tumbled out of his mouth that he didn't believe me. He stared at me hard, then critically, slowly shaking his head from side to side, as if he suspected I was drunk and had just told him some off-color joke.

"I'm telling you the truth," I said. "Go check for yourself."

Ramos stood, leisurely taking his time as if he knew this was a waste of a good afternoon. At that moment, Lacey came into the kitchen from the living room, where he'd been with his mother. He looked straight ahead past both of us, still holding the black knight in his hand, his talisman now, too.

"Are you the police? Mom said to tell you she was here, that she killed my stepmom with the stuff that is in that jar, and that she is sorry she did it," he said, pointing to the half-filled glass container of poisonous seeds. Lacey's distress left no doubt in Ramos's mind about the truth. He jumped off the kitchen stool, as if the words had hit him like blows, and stood up to face the boy.

"Come over here, son," he said, beckoning Lacey to come nearer. Ramos must have been a father himself or had the instincts of one. His face turned sad, and he threw his heavy arm around Lacey's shoulder, hugging him toward him. Lacey began to weep, collapsing into his hefty body and giving this seasoned detective every bit of sorrow he kept inside.

After comforting Lacey, Ramos ordered us back into the study and told us to close the door behind us. I assumed he was calling his office to send over reinforcements and the medical examiner, and I was right. Within ten minutes, the Osborne place was filled with officers from what looked like every rank and department. I could hear a few chatting in the kitchen and walking around in the living room. Most had probably gone to the upstairs bedroom where Mona's body lay. I checked the door to make sure it was closed tightly and would keep Lacey from hearing what was going on outside, but I assumed it would do little good. He was a smart kid and there was no way anything could shield him from what was going to happen.

After half an hour, I ventured back into the kitchen to get a sense of what was going on. There was only one officer there now, apparently guarding the premises. Because of what has become my peculiar relationship with the Grovesville police department, I recognized a familiar, if not a particularly friendly, face from last year. It was the no-nonsense officer who had reported to review another unexpected death scene that I'd inadvertently witnessed. I wondered if she remembered me, and hoped she wouldn't hold it against me. For some reason, I remembered her name, probably because it seemed to capture her so well. I approached her, taking a chance.

"Detective Doyle, I'm Dessa Jones, the person who made the call," I said, reintroducing myself.

Doyle was a no-nonsense woman with a no-nonsense style as blunt as her unfashionable haircut. She was a large woman who looked like Pilates and free weights were her reason for being; although her manner was gruff, her voice was surprisingly soft.

"First of all, I'm a sergeant, not a detective. It's Sergeant Doyle," she said with pride, quickly correcting me. "The detective is upstairs with the medical examiner and the body. He told me he wanted you and the child to stay put until Social Services got here for the kid. Where is the boy?"

I glanced behind to make certain that Lacey was still in the room. "His mother is the one who committed the crime."

"Oh my God! Are you serious? Is his father the one she killed?" Doyle asked, simple curiosity getting the better of her professional demeanor. She glanced back at the room as if expecting Lacey to make a sudden appearance.

"No. His father died a couple of weeks ago."

She made a low whistling sound and shook her head. "That's tough on the kid. Now his mom? What's that about?"

I didn't want to go into it again, so I shrugged as if I didn't know and tried to change the subject. "I have to tell you, I was really amazed how quickly you-all got here." She leaned toward me as if preparing to tell me something she probably shouldn't.

"Life can sure be ironic," she said instead.

"You have that right," I said, assuming she remembered who I was after all.

"We got here fast because we had been told to interview

the lady of the house, the one who is dead now. About . . . another matter," she said.

"Would that matter be the recently deceased Tyler Chase?" I watched her closely for a reaction, which told me I was right. She tried hard not to show it, but she was as bad a liar as me and the twitch of her left eyebrow gave her away.

"You should go back in there where the detective told you to stay until he calls Social Services for the kid and interviews you about what you know," she said, all business again.

I went back to check on Lacey, who was still holding the black knight and staring at the board as if waiting to move. He only looked up when the social worker entered the room and asked his name, and even then he just nodded without speaking. She was a thirtysomething short-haired blonde with horn-rimmed glasses that seemed too big for her face, but she had kind eyes and a gentle hand when she touched his shoulder and introduced herself as Sara. Detective Ramos stood behind her, as if to reassure Lacey he hadn't forgotten about him. Lacey gave him a nod but didn't look at me, not even when he and the social worker left.

Ramos interviewed me for the next hour or so for details about everything I knew and I told him what I could. He wrote everything down, asking about the glass container and when I'd first seen it. At last, he was through with me but said he might be in touch again in a week or so.

"By the way, the lady on the couch, the boy's mother, said she needed to ask you something before you left," he said as he was getting ready to go. "If you don't want to talk to her that's fine, but it seemed like it was important to her. Somebody has to watch out for that kid. Are you-all friends?"

"No, not for years."

"Well, suit yourself about talking, but whatever you do, make it fast."

I went back to Aurelia sitting on the couch, still covered

with dust from her garden, her dirty face now streaked with tears. It was hard to believe that this was the same Sunday, starting off as it had and ending now. Aunt Phoenix's words came back to me then; life was more twisted than simple, too quick and mysterious to know.

I didn't sit down next to Aurelia this time, just stood close enough to hear what she wanted to say.

"You asked me before about my son, well, that's what I want to ask you. Will you look out for him, for old times' sake?" she said.

I didn't answer for a while. She looked up, maybe scared I'd left without giving her my word. Or finally facing what was about to happen to her boy. I wasn't sure of that answer myself, but then I knew I had no choice. It was Darryl, of course, whispering in my ear, Rosemary, in her quiet way, and even Aunt Phoenix having her say.

"Yes, I will," I said because there was no other answer I could give.

I called Detective Ramos a week later to find out what was going to happen to Lacey. Aurelia Osborne pleaded guilty and would probably be in prison for a long time. Osborne's younger sister, who lived in a nearby city, had agreed to take Lacey in, but it would be a big adjustment. Ramos was reluctant to say much more but gave me the social worker's number and told me to talk to her. Lacey was a minor who had inherited a fortune. An attorney had been appointed by the court to protect him, but it would take concerned people with good intentions to make sure he was really okay. I was one of those people. Although I wasn't family, Lacey trusted me, and Ramos wanted my assurance that I'd look out for him.

It was a month before I talked to anybody about all that had happened. When I did, it was Lennox Royal in our favorite Chinese restaurant. There were things that still bothered me. Tyler Chase's murder was still unsolved, although the police were sure that Mona Osborne killed him. But that opened up questions about the death of her late husband, even though he had officially died of natural causes.

Lennox offered his thoughts about that as we were eating our Peking Duck.

"*Natural causes* simply means that it wasn't an accident or suicide and was related to his health. The death certificate would give more details," he said, deftly managing his chopsticks.

"He didn't look well when I saw him." It was a memory I didn't want to think about. I took a swallow of jasmine tea.

"The tragedy of being a detective is that you won't solve everything. Justice can be an elusive ideal." There was sadness in his eyes that I didn't see often. "Mona may have poisoned him subtly over months. She was a chemist, so she would know what to use. Maybe she never got over his role in her sister's suicide. You know the old saying that revenge is a dish best served cold, and in this case it was frozen.

"More likely, she wanted to inherit his money. Chase must have posed a threat to her. Why else would she kill him? But this is a heck of a thing to be talking about over dinner," he said, spreading a pancake with plum sauce and adding a sliver of duck. "If she's guilty, she paid the price. By the way, how is the newest member of your extended adopted family doing?"

"I've haven't adopted him, but he's definitely a member," I said, as eager as he was to change the subject.

"Along with Louella, Red, Erika, Harley—"

"Don't forget Tanya and Vinton," I added, and he chuckled. "So, Lennox, you actually do know everyone's name."

"Family is family," he said, offering me an egg roll.

"Lacey's aunt drops him by every week or so to visit. Things have been hard on him, but he's going to be okay."

"He definitely will as long as you're in his corner."

"He calls Erika his little sister, and she loves playing the role," I added, smiling at the thought.

"Bring him by the place to get some barbecue next time he comes over, and we'll play some chess."

"He'd love that. Whenever we play, he lets me win. He needs a challenge, and to be around some good men," I added more seriously.

"Most boys do. I know I did after my grandfather died."

We were lost in our thoughts as we finished dinner, me on Lacey and Lennox about parts of his life he wasn't yet ready to share. Suddenly, he looked up and grinned; I returned his smile. Meal by meal, we grew closer, and I wasn't quite sure if I was ready for that. Then I recalled the text my aunt had sent me early this morning. I'd dismissed it at first, but it came back now as I sat across from Lennox with that grin on his face. It was a Hausa proverb, one I hadn't seen before.

When the music changes, so should the dance.

As usual, Aunt Phoenix was right.

Dessa's Handy-Dandy Collard Greens Quiche

A tasty quiche is like an upright man—always have a good one on hand. This recipe comes with compliments to Jonell Nash, the late, great food editor of *Essence* magazine. I've added some touches of my own. Hopefully, Jonell would approve.

Basic piecrust for 9- or 10-inch pie pan (When I have time, I make my own crust, but store-bought is fine.)
4 large eggs
1 cup milk
½ teaspoon salt
½ teaspoon ground black pepper or cayenne pepper
½ teaspoon oregano
½ teaspoon nutmeg
¼ cup grated onion (sweet or red adds a nice touch!)
½ cup chopped red pepper
1½ cups chopped cooked fresh or frozen collard greens. Be sure to drain and squeeze them dry or your quiche will be watery.
½ to ¾ cup shredded Cheddar cheese

Heat oven to 375 degrees F for metal pan or 350 degrees for a glass pan. Roll out and ease pie dough into bottom and up sides of pie pan. Tuck edges under and crimp. Using a fork, prick bottom and sides. Partially bake for about 12 minutes until crust is beginning to color.

In a large bowl, lightly beat eggs and milk. Add salt, pepper, oregano, nutmeg, onion, red pepper, and collard greens and set aside.

Sprinkle half of cheese on piecrust. Pour egg mixture on top of cheese. Sprinkle remaining cheese on top. Bake until a knife inserted halfway between center and outside edge comes out clean, which is usually from 45 to 60 minutes. Let rest 10 minutes before cutting into wedges to serve.